THE
PLOUGHMEN

THE

PLOUGHMEN

A NOVEL

KIM ZUPAN

HENRY HOLT AND COMPANY   NEW YORK

Henry Holt and Company, LLC
Publishers since 1866
175 Fifth Avenue
New York, New York 10010
www.henryholt.com

Henry Holt® and 🙶® are registered trademarks of
Henry Holt and Company, LLC.

Library of Congress Cataloging-in-Publication Data
Zupan, Kim
    The ploughmen : a novel / Kim J. Zupan.—First edition.
        pages   cm
    ISBN 978-0-8050-9951-5 (hard cover)—ISBN 978-0-8050-9952-2 (electronic book)
1. Murderers—Fiction.   2. Police—Fiction.   3. Intimacy (Psychology)—
Fiction.   4. Montana—Fiction.   5. Psychological fiction.   I. Title.
    PS3626.U63P56 2014
    813'.6—dc23   2013025013

Henry Holt books are available for special promotions and
premiums. For details contact: Director, Special Markets.

First Edition 2014

Designed by Kelly S. Too

Printed in the United States of America
1   3   5   7   9   10   8   6   4   2

To Bill and Virginia Zupan.

And to Janet.

For we are strangers before thee, and sojourners,
as were all our fathers: our days on the earth are as a shadow,
and there is none abiding.

—1 CHRONICLES 29:15

THE
PLOUGHMEN

PROLOGUE

The boy got off the bus at the end of the dry lane in the fall of the year, the shelterbelt as he shuffled past shirring with the sound of grasshoppers that wheeled crazily out of the weeds and dusty pale leaves of the Russian olives, blundering into his pants legs, careening off his shirtfront. One day a month he and his schoolmates were released early and encouraged to use the time to perform Corporal Works of Mercy. Val was a serious boy. He shifted his books from hand to hand as he walked toward the far house and began to list them: visit the sick, clothe the naked, bury the dead. What others? The neighbor's black cattle from the bluff looked down, their shapes swimming and wandering eerily in the heat haze. Visit those in prison, that was one. Give drink to those who thirst. To the west he could see his father on the Minneapolis-Moline circling the Schmidt field in a cirrus of dust below the bluff.

His mother's handwriting was a lustrous script perfected under the scowls and flailing yardsticks of the same forbidding Sisters of Providence who now taught him—the notes left in his lunch box or in the margins of a birthday card or, on the rare occasions she and his father went out, he found on his pillow—keepsakes to be hoarded. There was care in the rendering of the loop and slant of her letters as if, like words chiseled in a temple frieze, they were meant to last a thousand years. On this September day the note stood upright between salt and pepper shakers in the shape of smiling pigs. *Darling—Come alone to the shed.*

He went into his younger sister's room and she lay sleeping under rumpled sheets with her thumb in her mouth. He took an apple from a bowl by the sink and stood at the counter eating it. Through the window across the gravelly lot he could see the shed door standing open. A meadowlark lit atop the lone yard-light pole, warbled, flew. He stood staring after it. In a month it would be gone.

In the yard, dust rose beneath his feet and the day was bright. In town, his friends were playing tag on the green boulevards but his place, he knew, was here. The door to the shed swayed on its hinges groaning and what he could see of the interior was only darkness. A single cloud in the brilliant firmament towed its image across the ground miles away. She would have stopped to watch it go.

For years they'd kept chickens in the metal pole barn, an enterprise she had said was a losing battle, as those that did not simply freeze to death fell victim to fox or skunk and if she was going to be in the business of feeding every predator in the country she'd just go ahead and buy dog food and be done with it. The chickens had been gone a long while, yet when the wind blew and the building shuddered under it, feathers still drifted down from the purlins and collar ties all but invisible high above in the murk of shadow. Now as he stood inside, arms around a rough post, one such filthy snowflake fell in random drift and he could see in the gloom overhead the rope looped twice and tied.

Later he remembered the smell of the chickens there and he imagined them in the dim recesses bobbing their scabrous heads and clawing the gravel with their horrible feet. He remembered these things and that her hand when he finally touched it felt like the wood of the post he gripped so tightly, watching in the dusty fug the slow slow metronomic swaying of her body.

He righted the ladder from where it had fallen, ascended the steps as she had and sawed at the rope for a long time with his pocketknife. With a bespattered grain tarp he covered her where she fell, dust rising from its folds in the stifling air like a sprite, and he touched her leg once to assure himself that she was wooden now, was not his mother but some other thing left in her place.

He stepped into the brilliant doorway, turned briefly. His outsized shadow lay across the floor and across the tarp and leaned aslant on the wall in a scarecrow parody of himself. He considered his work and it was not right. He went once more across the ranchyard to the house, rummaged in a closet in her room. He checked on his sister, swept back a damp curl from her face, laid a hand on her narrow back to feel the timorous swelling of life there and went out again across the gravel to the shed carrying the box. He pulled back the tarp and stood looking down at the naked feet.

Afterward he rearranged the tarp, tucking it carefully. He leaned the ladder against the wall and smoothed the dirt with his foot where he had knelt and then had walked across the shorn fields and summerfallow toward the cloud of dust with his father inside it. He stopped once to look back at what his life had been and then kept walking.

"It was a mistake," his father said. "That note was for me." If theirs had been a different marriage it might have been an invitation to a tryst but he would have known. He would have known it was not. "She forgot you'd get home early. It was all just an awful goddamn mistake."

The boy didn't hear or didn't believe and he stood staring at the dirty toes of his school shoes. He had been summoned. In the sensuous cursive of his mother's hand he had been given responsibility. He would not relinquish it.

"I don't understand." His father could not stop shaking his head. He made a strangled sound. He hadn't touched her. He hadn't touched the boy. "She hated those slippers." He looked at the boy and the boy looked away. The boy thought, How do you not understand? It was simple: it was for me to do. I was her Valentine.

"It don't make sense," his father said. "She never wore them once."

ONE

As if to fend off a blow he threw up his arms in front of his face and the first bullet went through his thin forearm and through the top half of his right ear and went whirring into the evening like a maddened wasp. The next as he turned to run took him high in the back of the neck and he fell headlong and did not move. The old man went to him and examined the wound critically. He turned the boy over. The bullet had come out below his nose and the old man considered its work, while the boy batted his eyes and took in the sky beyond the killer's bland and placid face—gray clouds of failing winter, a small black leaf, a black kite, at last an enormous wheel of March's starlings, descending with the mere sound of breath.

From where he sat, the old man could see the river, the white-caps and the pitching gulls indistinguishable, and he could see the tallest buildings of the old smelterworks beyond the coulee's steep flanks and in the east the shadowed Missouri Breaks raggedly diminishing into the hazy blue gloaming of coming spring. He could feel the last of winter in the wind, see it in the color of the river, gray and churning like molten lead.

The soil there was poor and sandy and the grass on those slopes grew sporadically and reminded him of pigs' hair. There were yucca and prickly pear and he could hear like a faint voice in his ear the hiss of blowing soil at the ridge crest. Still a farmer, he thought. He sifted the dirt through his fingers. The slope below was nearly bare and troughed by the melt-off of ten thousand springtimes. Still a goddamn farmer. Seed put down here would most likely just wash away. Scattered about lay cobbles of sandstone, spalls of shale like medieval roof tiles randomly shingling the slanted ground. A gull came near enough that above the wind and the sea-spray hiss he could hear its thin woman-cry. He looked up briefly, then called to the young man below him in the coulee bottom. "Deeper," he said. "You got to make it deeper."

The man looked up and leaned on his shovel handle briefly and then continued to dig.

"Hear me?" he said.

"I hear you." The younger man was sweating and had thrown aside his jacket, its arms twisted among the brittle weeds.

He watched the digger assail the dirt ineffectually, then raised his eyes to the broken landscape below him. He liked this place. He had used it before and that comforted him. It was like a warehouse he knew well and that was there when he needed it, quiet and close to town. The dirt was poor but there were few rocks and the digging was easy. Boys came to this side of the river in the early fall to sight in their rifles for hunting season. The sound of gunfire was not unusual. At the head end of nearly every coulee lay boxes with targets taped to them, and brass shell casings lay about everywhere as though a series of battles had raged down the ravines and over the low divides and sere hills.

Shortly the other man laid aside his shovel and waited and then the two of them rolled the body in and they began covering it over, one with the shovel, the other, the farmer, because he still held the blunt pistol, pushing in the soil with the side of his foot.

The wind swept momentarily down into the raw gulch and the hair on the older man's balding pate stood straight up. The gull circled, calling into the pale blue sky where immane banks of cloud raced toward low mountains in the south, bound to the stratosphere by filaments of distant rain. The older man, whose name was John Gload, stooped to pick up a grain sack which held in its bottom the severed hands and head of the young man whose body they'd just consigned to the thin and unproductive soil of the Missouri River Breaks. Anonymous bones now, among others—John Gload's dark signature on the landscape of the world.

Two hundred years earlier, the wayfarers under Lewis and Clark had portaged over this very ground, trundling their boats in the heat around the impassable falls. Gload, never voluble when he was at work, remembered that bears had once lived here and the thought made him smile.

"Bears," he said. "Grizzly bears, right here."

The younger man looked at him uncomprehendingly.

"Don't give me that look," Gload said. "I'm trying to teach you something. Used to run around here like gophers. Hundred fifty years ago they would of had this asshole dug up and ate before we got over the hill." The older man pointed up the slope where dun cheatgrass sawed about under the March wind, imagined there old silvertips a-totter on their hind legs like lethal storybook ogres, sorting out the scent of them. "Course they might of got us, too." He held the small pistol flat in his palm and considered it. "This goddamn thing wouldn't do nothing but put a little spring in their step while they ripped your head off." Gload surveyed the country round, imagining the hills alive with such beasts. He ran his eyes up and down his thin partner appraisingly. "You wouldn't make more than a bitty turd-pile."

They walked then down along the flat coulee bottom, the younger man with the shovel over his shoulder like an infantryman. They stepped among bluestem and sagebrush, bottle shards glistering in the silt like gemstones, and passed without note the stripped bone cages of the poached and butchered deer of the previous fall.

The younger man who now drove the car was named Sidney White and was called by all who knew him Sid the Kid. Though he had never sat a horse or been among cows he thought himself a cowboy and his fabrication was one of snap-button shirt and tight jeans stogged into a pair of secondhand boots a size and a half too large, the uppers gaudily colored and stamped with flowers and elaborate glyphs and tooled with the initials of the previous owner. He was vain of his lank black hair combed back slick, and so eschewed the addition of a hat to his costumery. John Gload had found him through a series of dismaying defaults and in the end had used him simply because of his youth and apparent good teeth, which the old man judged indicated an abstinence from methamphetamine. This was Sid White's first real score and he was excited.

As they drove, White suggested they turn north on an

intersecting gravel road which would take them in fifteen minutes' time to a house set among the strips of vast wheat farms
north of town that had indeed once been a farmhouse but had
in recent years been home to an older woman and her three
younger charges.

"You know the place? It ain't but ten miles." He wrung the
steering wheel, agitated, swung his narrow eyes from the curv-
ing river road to John Gload and back again. "I say we cap things
off with a little trim."

Gload stared at the river through a verge of leafless willows
and the water frothed under the wind. The gulls he so despised
hung against the gray crepe of the spring sky like Japanese paper
sculpture pinned there.

"No," he said.

"You don't know it?"

"I know it. And no is the answer."

"This here's the turn coming up." Sid White slowed. Perhaps the old man might change his mind. The unmarked road,
little more than parallel ruts with a hemstitch of wheat stubble,
aspired gently northward and seemed to vanish, gone at this
evening hour the frontier between summerfallow earth, summerfallow sky.

Gload sighed and turned to regard the kid's profile, an acne-
pitted hawk's face with a profusion of ragged blue-black Indian
hair. "We're not going there just so you can remind yourself that
you're better than the thing you just put in a hole."

The kid looked at him. "What you talkin' 'bout?"

"That's why you feel like you need to get laid. It's no more
than that."

"Bro, that ain't true. I live for that poontang. Anytime, anywhere."

"And don't talk that fake ghetto talk around me. You're no spade."

"Whatever, man."

"Yes. Whatever."

They went past the turn and drove for a time in silence. John Gload brushed at a stain on his trousers. On their left the river had turned the color of wine, the stone bluffs on the far shore in the sudden shadows turned to statuary—dour countenances, creatures seen in dreams.

Sidney White said finally, "Might of done you some good, though. It relieves tension, sex does, and I ain't making it up because I read that somewheres."

"Do I look tense to you?" Gload said. "Do I appear tense?"

The kid glanced over at him and then began to slowly nod his head. His small teeth, revealed in a leer, were brilliant. "Okay," he said. "All right. They got stuff for that. I could hook you up, pard."

The older man appeared not to have heard, an unaccustomed uneasiness at that moment creeping into his limbs. When he was a boy, once, sitting on a bald and rocky hillside in the early dark, a bat came so near he felt the air beside his face move and it left him with a chill of foreboding that had little to do with the October evening. It was a stirring much like that he felt now in the still interior of the car. He looked to see that the windows were rolled up and that the heater's fan was off, and he glanced at the kid to see if it was some trick, some sleight of hand.

White caught the look. Sensing some interest he said, "That's right. Your old lady would be plumb wore out."

He'd been thinking about her even before the kid conjured her image, how in bed her slim leg would be draped across his own as though to maintain a connection even in sleep, as if not touching him even that near was to be utterly apart.

John Gload, as if to pat the kid on the shoulder, raised his left arm from the seat back where it rested and put the short barrel of the gun to the kid's ear. The kid drew in his breath and held it.

"I don't need nothing," Gload said.

"Okay."

"Don't ever talk to me about this kind of shit again. You understand? You don't know nothing about me and never will." The kid nodded very slowly, as if afraid even this vague movement might ignite death in his ear. As an afterthought Gload said, "And none of that bullshit jailyard talk, either."

The kid drove, pouting, until Gload told him to stop. He pulled the car onto the shoulder of the road and sat smoking while Gload got out and began shifting the contents of the trunk behind the raised lid. Then he could hear the hatchet working. He dandled his wrist atop the steering wheel and stared out broodingly at an outlandish sky, long flaming celestial mesas and reefs and the copper half disk of the sun diminishing beyond stagecraft mountains in the west and sucking after it, into that far void, minute birds the color of embers. The chopping sound from the rear of the car went on rhythmically—chunk, chunk, chunk.

In the side-view mirror he watched Gload walk to the rocky shoreline and throw something into the murky chop. The gulls, substantiating from seeming nowhere, began to dive and keen while John Gload waved his arms about like a conjurer. He stooped and threw handfuls of gravel. The kid watched this in the mirror and finally turned in the seat to watch out the window and when Gload came back the kid was smiling.

"You can't never hit nothing with just rocks."

The old man favored the kid briefly with a bland look and settled into his seat without replying. The kid shrugged, levered the car into gear, and drove west on the narrow blacktop, in the windshield the sun a tangerine shard wedged among the distant black peaks.

"A shotgun, now," White said. "That'd get your point acrost."

They went in silence toward the garish sunset and then Gload said, "Pull over at the dam."

"Hell, it'll be dark here pretty quick."

Gload ignored him. "Pull over up here." Sid eased the car into a pullout for utility company vehicles, at the head of a long set of wooden stairs descending to gloom. "Pop the trunk and wait here," Gload said.

The kid watched him go down the stairs with the grain sack. Below, the lights along the great curve of the dam began to flicker on. Presently he saw John Gload appear in the first circle of light and fade and reappear in the next, progressing this way along the concrete catwalk, incorporeal as a phantom.

A fine spray rose above the dam's railings from the torrent roaring through the floodgates and when Gload finally stopped it appeared as a downy luminescent cloud above his head. He stood at the rail and watched the amber water of spring thaw surge through the sluicegates. He turned. Behind him in the curve of the dam, tree limbs wheeled about in a huge scum-covered whirlpool, rising and falling like the arms of drowning giants. Half-inflated plastic grocery bags like men-of-war bobbed in the wrack and there were animals so terribly bloated that they may have been cats or hogs and he could make out the dented prow of a skiff and there was all manner of floatable trash and slim branches fluted by beaver teeth and there were

ducks and small waterbirds, their dead eyes gemlike in the glare
and everywhere in the slime like a grotesque choir the round
sucking mouths of voracious river carp.

Gload turned and strode across the concrete walkway and
dropped the sack into a great spout of water and it shot forward
and past the brief yellow corona and was gone. On that ancient
riverbed were the bones of fish long extinct the size of dolphins
and there were the bones of plesiosaurs and mastodons and the
disjoined skeletons of luckless Cree and Blackfeet two centuries
old. Standing in the dark interstice between the spillway lights,
Gload felt connected with history, a part of a greater plan. For
all that, he took no chances. He had taken the young man's
hands and chopped the teeth from his head and with these now
settling on the river bottom the corpse was as nameless as the
fossilized bones of preadamite fish.

When he got back to the car, Sid the Kid was asleep sitting
up with his hands on the wheel, a cigarette smoldering above
his knuckle. Gload stood outside smoking and waiting and then
the kid began to yowl and shake his hand and stuck two fingers
in his mouth. Gload slid in on the passenger side, shaking his
head.

"Take me home," he said. "Tomorrow we go get rid of the
stuff."

Amber leaves of the previous fall lay pooled beneath the apple
trees, thin and black against the gunmetal sky. A covey of Hungarian partridge scuttled across the weedy lot, articulated like a
tiny train, in the window's light the males' ruby throatbands
flashing an electric brilliancy amid all the dun color of the wild
grass. In that yellowed rectangle he could see Francie pass and
repass. The chimney issued bone-white smoke that stood in the

strangely still air as rigid and substantial as a church spire. As he watched her, the uneasiness once more fluttered past. He batted the air beside his head as though it were a living thing.

He had walked the half mile up his drive from the county road where he'd had the kid drop him and now he stood among his trees smoking. Though the river was two miles away its smell was on the air and it was faintly perfumed by the sage on the benchlands that lay just to the south.

Once in a drought year a bear had come, shambling down from the Highwood Mountains twenty miles distant, and taken up residence in the grove, eating the fallen bitter little apples and sleeping there unabashed on the ground amid the brittle leaves and rimed grass and leaving like spilled preserves huge piles of his shit everywhere. In the end he took to climbing the trees for the few apples that would not fall and at night from their bed they could hear the small knurred branches crack under his weight with the sound of distant fireworks. Gload had left it alone, seeing in its shape and nature something of himself.

When he'd gone in and poured coffee into his favorite cup and sat at the table, she said, "Do I look any better through a window than I do in person?" She had turned from her work, smiling, swirling ice in the glass she held.

"You won't sing when I'm in the room. I like your singing."

"I could have you run in for spying on a lady like that."

"For a hell of a lot more than that," he said.

From behind the kitchen counter she approached him a little unsteadily and she laid a soft, cool hand alongside John Gload's face. She stared down into his eyes, dark wells wherein such things existed that he could not tell her or anyone. And as if she glimpsed some of what was there she said, "There's some

good in you, Johnny. And I might be the only one knows it."
Gload's hands lay on either side of his cup and she took her hand
from his face and placed it atop one of his. He looked down at
them wordlessly. It might have been what he loved most about
her, that she seemed to know some things, horrible things, but
she forgave him them and this small act—of laying her smooth
hand atop his own, which had so recently held the bloodied
instruments of his trade—was a sort of absolution.

"I got to leave tomorrow. For a few days."

"I ought to know the pattern by now. So we'll eat a nice dinner and watch the TV and go to bed early."

"That would be nice."

"Am I allowed to ask when you'll be back?"

"Sure you can ask, but I don't know. Three, four days."

"What if one time you don't come back? Me out here all by
myself? I couldn't do it. For a few days I'm okay. But even a week
is getting to be too hard, Johnny."

"I always come back. Have I never not come back?"

"If you never did come back we wouldn't be talking right
now about you coming back."

John Gload extricated his hand from under hers, a quavering translucent bird of a hand, and cupped his own brutal paws
over his ears.

"Let's eat," he said. "You're making my head hurt."

They ate a long leisurely meal and Francie for her dessert
drank two glasses of port wine in a jam jar and as was their long
habit sat at the side door listening to the evening sounds and
watching the western sky flame and slowly transubstantiate to
an ebony velvet arrayed with shards of quartz. They went to bed
and made love on the cool sheets with the windows opened
slightly to a cross breeze. Pale skin, pale sheets—beneath him

she seemed a being fading from view, the look she wore, so dreamy and distant, as if like a person going down slowly down in a lake, she watched the cruel surface recede with bemused carelessness. Before John Gload's heartbeats subsided Francie was asleep and softly snoring and he lay listening to miller moths battering themselves on the window screen behind his head—small souls seeking the freedom of the greater world. Recently he'd begun to imagine Francie's spirit fluttering among them.

He could not sleep but neither did he want to get out of bed. She would not wake up, he knew, because she slept as deeply as a child, but he hated to be far from her when he knew he was leaving. So he lay in the dark. She slept on her back composed as if by an undertaker, even to her white hands crossed on her small breasts, though one leg stretched out to rest against his. A tether, a lifeline. The wind shifted the thin curtains and rattled the curtain rings on the brass rod that held them and in the neglected orchard beside the house an owl called. Some long time later, with her breathing close at his ear and the curtains like pale spirits hovering at the edge of his sight, he slept. He had been imagining a long-ago field and he rode the plow around and around in that dreamy sunlight.

TWO

It was dark among the trees and when the young man came into a clearing the snow lay deep and untrammeled, lit softly blue from the quarter moon and the stars swarming in the cloudless vault above the peaks. After a while the boles of the ponderosa and lodgepole revealed themselves from the blackness and then soon the lower branches hung with moss like hag's hair, and small birds began to rouse and dart out before them like vanguards. The small stream he followed muttered beneath a thin pane of ice and among the topmost branches of the trees a faint wind was another secret voice and he stopped to listen. He peered ahead to the black rampart of timber. Maybe today, he thought. Maybe it will be today.

It was the first week in April and the deputy sheriff and his dog tracked a young woman separated from her skiing companions during a brief and vicious early spring storm at a forked drainage in the Crazy Mountains. A night and a day and another

night had passed and on the following morning Valentine
Millimaki on snowshoes set out from the trailhead in frigid
darkness.

In the course of his duties with the Copper County Sheriff's
Department he spent time investigating rural crimes and he
endured his required hours in the old jail building adjacent to
the county courthouse, a grim edifice of sandstone blocks hewn
by Croatian masons which in its earliest days had held cattle rus-
tlers and horse thieves. But it was work outdoors that he loved,
with the three-year-old shepherd dog tracking through the
woods and brush and sudden canyons in wildlands where maps
of some blank and forgotten corners were still mere suggestions
of one's place in the world.

Some he found scratched and bruised or limping aimlessly
atop a fractured ankle with a tree branch for a crutch, some in the
late stages of hypothermia doddering half-naked through drifts in
pursuit of ghosts and visions. Hunters, hikers, felons afoot from
stolen vehicles at the dead ends of logging roads. All alive. Thir-
teen months ago he'd found an autistic child, scratched and shivering in the timber in the rain with his lapdog clinched beneath
his arm like a shabby carnival prize, limp and strangled. That had
been the last. For over a year now there had been only bodies.

The dog was working well, lunging with difficulty through
the heavy snow, and Millimaki told him so. "Good Tom. Find
the girl." The shepherd stopped to look at him, his tongue already
hanging long from his mouth, and he lapped once at the snow
and went on.

Millimaki halted briefly to examine new tracks quartering
across their path. Prints of deer stove into the virgin snow,
overlaid with those of a big cat. The hair along the dog's back
rose and his lip turned back quivering to show his gleaming

teeth and Millimaki spoke to him again. Other tracks atop the new snow, hieroglyphics of mice and squirrels—frantic senseless diasporas into the perilous open where owls swept down spectral and silent as the night itself. Today, Millimaki thought again. Our luck may change today.

Some ten miles in she lay on her back in a trail under a dusting of new snow with a topographical map spread atop her chest as if in her bed she had fallen asleep reading. Tom sat on his haunches at the side of the trail cocking his ears at Millimaki, who squatted beside the woman, brushing away the snow from her face. He sat looking at her, so white, white as porcelain, her blue lips drawn tight as though in deep concentration, but for all that a peaceful sylvan sleeper, her skis and poles arrayed beside her neatly to be taken up after that brief consultation of the map.

The day was utterly silent and brilliant now, the sun at that hour straight overhead and the sky above the clearing where the woman had stopped was galleried by a coven of ghostly pinetops. Perhaps she'd stood gazing uncomprehendingly at the emerging stars, in their milky light superimposing the enormous order wheeling overhead onto the map that seemed to hold her life in its obtuse loops and lines. Perhaps she would lie down and from that vantage Polaris might appear, or another far sun that could reinstate her in the paradoxical world. For just a moment, a few short minutes. The unknowable stars looking down. A brief nap in the clearing in the starlight.

These are the things Valentine Millimaki imagined. A small bird came to sit on the branch of a tree and took in the scene—dog, man, statue—then flew. He watched it disappear into the sun. The young woman had lost a mitten and her bare hand lay atop the map. Wearing the snowshoes, Millimaki squatted with some difficulty. The dog sat watching him. He removed his own mitten and extended his hand and touched her wrist. As he touched all of them. What remained, he told himself, was not what they had been.

He stood and considered the long trek out and eventual return leg after hours of delay while protocol was satisfied. His day was just begun. His ungloved hand was numb and pale and he stood thwacking it clublike against his leg, the whop whop whop unreasonably loud in the sepulchral stillness. The dog looked at him quizzically. He said, "Let's go, Tom." The dog stood and circled once and looked from him to the woman in the snow. She slept on. "Come on. She's all right now."

Fifteen hours later, at home in his bed, Millimaki thought again of the woman sleeping alone beneath her cold white counterpane in the woods. His wife had stirred when he crawled in beside her, the chill still gripping his bones, phantom pack straps furrowing his back.

"I'm home," he whispered. He shifted closer for the warmth of her, for the life in her. "I found her."

"What?" She spoke from the edge of a dream, her words slurred. "Who?"

"The woman I was after, in the Crazies."

"That's good." From far away, barely audible, she said, "That's nice."

"I didn't get there in time." In the darkness above his head he was seeing the woman again, blanched and rigid. "I didn't make it."

He'd wanted his wife to say she was sorry, that this epidemic of woodenness would soon end. That the next one would be alive and breathing and grateful. To say, "It wasn't your fault, Val. It's not ever your fault."

"Oh, Val," she said, "Please. Go to sleep. I need to sleep."

He put his hand on his wife's warm back and soon he felt through the heave of her ribs the slow rhythm of sleep. After a long while he slept. A wind out of the prairies of Alberta rattled the branches of the box elder trees against the house eaves and the cabin door shuddered in its jamb. It blew and drifted deep all night and the country in the clear blue dawn would be new and immaculate and anything lost in it would be lost until there was little to be found but bones.

He had saved her from that. He had done that at least.

The day following was Monday and after four scant hours of shallow sleep he dressed in the dark to not wake his wife. Lying beside her he was visited that night by the dream that in recent weeks was never far away. In it his mother's mouth was not blue like the woman's he had found earlier nor did it look as it did when as a boy he'd found her but was instead painted the color of cherries or of blood, horrible against the white of her doll's-face.

Palsied and leaden he drove the blank white country through the coming dawn to assume his shift as court security for the old man who had recently taken up residence in the Copper County jail. The hills' incipient green, so faint and tenuous it may have been merely a trick of the eye after months of white on gray, was utterly erased by the storm. Songbirds gathered stunned and mute in the cottonwoods along the creek and on the right-of-way fence wires and the roadway was smeared and littered with gore, deer come to feed on weeds exposed by the county's plows grotesquely disassembled by tractor trailers careening through the dark toward Billings and Cheyenne. Millimaki stopped once to drag a young doe from the centerline of

the highway, among the gray and glistening ropes of her umbles
a tiny fawn spilling from its caul. Crows and magpies swarmed
the humming powerlines overhead, awaiting the tender carrion and greeting with caws and croaks the plenitude of the
refulgent day.

The day they'd gone for him, one week earlier, was a day so
fine that Millimaki drove with his window rolled down, the
ruddy road dust from the patrol car in front of him that seeped
into the cab of little consequence because it made him believe
in the possibility of spring.

The old man stood up from his chair as if to greet old friends.
Millimaki walked down the short length of road behind the
other men as instructed, Dobek advancing with his piece drawn
and aimed at the man's midsection, Wexler beside him with the
shotgun, the barrel wandering dangerously as he quick-stepped
through the grass grown up in the center of the lane. It was a
mild day but Dobek's shaved head gleamed with sweat. Wexler
was pale, his prominent adam's apple jerking in his throat.

Dobek called out as they approached, "Sit in the chair, asshole." Gload showed his hands front and back like a magician
and resumed his seat.

"Now on your feet." Dobek and Wexler stopped ten feet
short, their guns upraised. They were breathing hard as if they'd
run a great distance. The old man put his hands on his thighs
and rose with an air of detachment or boredom, unconcerned
with the two black boreholes wavering lethally in front of him,
his eyes instead searching the pale blue vault above in the direction of the river where he seemed to be expecting something to
appear.

"Down on the fucking ground."

"Up, down, up, down," the old man said.

"Down in the fucking dirt, now," Dobek bellowed. "Hands behind. Millimaki, get the bracelets on him." Millimaki knelt and snapped the handcuffs in place. They were barely large enough to fit over the old man's massive wrists, only two teeth of the ratchet end engaging the pawl.

Dobek, his round smooth dome gleaming, stood off several feet with his sidearm leveled at the old man's broad back. One of the older deputies on the force, he wore a tailored uniform that now fit too tightly across his gut, and the short sleeves he favored revealed a faded USMC tattoo on one biceps and on the other some snarling animal—wolf or panther—it, too, indistinct, whether from age or maladroit artistry, but its message of predation was clear. He was an enforcer, a departmental bogeyman to be conjured when all reason failed to mollify prisoners gone mad in their cages. Now he motioned with his chin and the two younger men got Glood to his feet and Wexler began patting him down. In his agitated state he'd leaned the scattergun carelessly against the chair's seat where it teetered, and Millimaki stepped around him and took it up and punched the safety on. Wexler ran his hands up and down the old man's faded shirt and beneath his arms and moved to his feet, slapping and chopping up the bowed legs and finally leering up at the two other men as he squeezed the old man's genitals, saying, "Nothing."

"Who's inside?" Dobek asked.

"No need to holler. I can hear as good as you."

"I said, Who's inside, goddamn it."

"Nobody."

"Nobody's ass. We'll see." Dobek nodded to Wexler, who took up the shotgun, and they moved toward the rear door of

the house. "Millimaki, keep your piece on this fuck." He jerked
the screen door open savagely and nodded Wexler to the fore
and they banged through the main door in combat positions.
The screen door, weather-checked and paintless, hung askew,
the top hinge screws pulled nearly loose.

Gload had watched them enter his house and when he turned
to Millimaki he wore an expression of deep sadness. "Now look
what they done to that door."

"That can be fixed easy enough."

"It's got some dry rot. You got to be gentle with it."

Millimaki said, "Is anyone here?"

"Like I said, nobody."

The deputy brushed the dirt and grass from the old man's
shirtfront and trousers and brought forward the chair for him
to sit. Millimaki turned and looked at the wild orchard where
spring was foretold by minute buds and the presence of tiny
birds among the brambles. He noted crocuses in bloom along
the walk and bright yellow flowers turned toward the sun.

"What are these?" he said. "Daffodils?"

The old man shrugged. He'd begun to watch the young deputy with interest.

Millimaki turned his back to the old man and studied the
tangle of trees. "You might have wanted to cut these trees back
without any mercy. It's out of control in there."

The old man stared at him with his mouth ajar.

Millimaki said, "What kind of apples are they?"

"Couldn't tell you," Gload said.

Millimaki ducked into the trees and, reaching to a high
branch, picked an apple from the previous year that had somehow not fallen, shrunken and hard as ornamental fruit. He
rolled it in his palms, sniffed it. Around him the small birds

swirled, their tiny black eyes following his every move. John Gload watched him. He looked to the young man in the trees and he glanced at the door of his house where the two deputies had gone and he looked down the narrow lane to the county road beyond.

Millimaki came out of the trees. "Best guess is they're some kind of old McIntosh," he said.

Before the old man could reply, Dobek and Wexler banged out of the house, the older deputy at ease now and smirking and eating a pear he'd found inside. When he saw the two other men conversing, the older man sitting cross-legged in his chair, Millimaki once again examining the apple, the pear exploded out of his mouth. He sputtered, "Christ, Millimaki, I said put your piece on him. Did I not say that?" He'd holstered his sidearm and now he had it out again and pointed at the old man in the chair. "Wexler, did I not say to him, Put your piece on this piece of shit?"

"You did, Voyle. Definitely."

"The fuck's the matter with you?"

"Cuffed and sitting in a chair," Millimaki said. "Where's he gonna go?"

"Fuck." Dobek looked from the young deputy to the old man, who placidly sat in his chair, cocking his long equine head carelessly to the trills and frantic fluttering of the springtime birds in his arbor. The old man's insouciance seemed to enrage the veteran deputy and the flesh of his neck bulged above his uniform collar red as a coxcomb. "Fuck," he said again. Wexler's small blue eyes swung from Dobek to Gload and to Dobek again, reading the veteran's face. He raised the scattergun to his waist, his finger massaging the trigger guard nervously. With his free hand Dobek thumbed a line of sweat from his forehead and slung it to the side.

"There was a time not all that long ago when we'd of just dropped a rope over something or other and been done with this suvabitch. But now." He surveyed with clouded countenance the country around them for all its corruption and inefficacy, the weak imperfect world an insult to him. "Now we got to go through the whole song and dance and the spending of taxpayer money and feeding this suvabitch for ten or fifteen or however too many years to wind up with the same exact thing—a dead fucker hanging."

Wexler smiling, nodding. "Fucking right, Voyle."

John Gload throughout this gazed off wistfully toward the low hills that rose to the north, where juniper and scrub pine grew on stubbornly among the weeds and sage. Great shoals of cumulus scudding on the wind. Dobek stepped up from behind and ran the barrel of his pistol roughly along the old man's bristled cheek, eliciting a sandpaper sound. With the cold nickel barrel he traced the curve of the old man's ear. When Gload snatched his large head to the side Dobek stepped back as if scalded.

Once more he troweled sweat from his forehead. "Okay," he said. "All right. Where's the woman of the house, old man."

"Not here."

"I deduced that all on my very own, asshole. Where'd she go?"

"Just gone," Gload said. "Gone off."

Dobek stood for a moment, tapping his handgun against the stripe of his uniform pants. He exchanged a look with Wexler then turned to Millimaki, his obsidian eyes lingering there longer as if considering his options. Finally he said, "Okay, Wexler, get him in the car. And I want the footwear on him, too."

John Gload's expression never changed as he was jerked

erect and pushed toward the car. He glanced once at the house and once longingly at the wild bosk of trees and he looked briefly to the sky to the south where skeins of thin cirrus mirrored the slow river below. His eyes too swung across Millimaki, who'd stood aside carefully among the radiant spring blooms to let the other two lead the old man away to his fate.

The corridor of cells was belowground and the darkness stayed long there, the sickly purple-blue light from the hissing fluorescents and the light that came in through the two high windows scant at any hour, any season. The snow had begun to melt and water poured from the downspouts of the old building and overran the gutters, cascading down the sandstone block and over the street-level windows in myriad rills. From within, the glass appeared to run and shift like mercury.

The night jailer at the end of his shift walked with Millimaki as if in a trance down the dank corridor and introduced him to the old man and turned and retraced his steps and went out into the light of the new day, which he seemed altogether unsuited for. His eyes were so red and the circles under them so dark, he seemed to be wearing thespian's makeup and the flesh seen above his collar and below his shirt cuffs had the yellow cast of a consumptive.

Because of his age and reputation and the nature of his crimes John Gload was kept out of the bullpen and housed in one of the county jail's hospital cells, different from the six other county jail cages of the general population only in that it was separated from them by a short hallway and a locking door. In the course of his long career the old man had inhabited such lodgings before. As a much younger man he had done ten years in the state penitentiary in Rawlins, Wyoming, much of it in solitary confinement, and on an overhead water pipe in that cell he had done thousands of pull-ups, the only sounds for hours in the near-profound dark his breathing and the mouselike whinge-ing of the pipe protesting his weight. His arms, even at the age of seventy-seven, were so large that when he extended his hand toward Millimaki he could only get it through the bars just beyond the wrist.

Gload had come forward, his face lit for an instant by the overheads and the aqueous niggardly light the high windows afforded and then receding to shadow.

"We've met," Millimaki said. "Informally, I guess you'd say."

From beyond the lightfall he heard Gload say, "I recanize you from the welcoming committee. The apple expert."

Millimaki drew up a chair from the opposite wall of the nar-row hallway and sat. They waited for the call to move across the street to the courthouse. The cells beyond the sally gate were quiet—men asleep, men absent, in court themselves shackled and fearful and sweating in their issue coveralls. Men in their cages atop their bunks biding oppressive time, urgently listening to any voices but those inside their heads.

"It's a nice place you have out there," Millimaki said. "Hope you don't mind I poked around a bit after you went to town."

"Why would I mind? Nothing to hide."

"Good soil. Out of the wind, for the most part. Nice little spot."

Gload nodded. "I appreciate that." Small sounds came from the dark—a striking match, the noise of a tin can sliding. Blue smoke substantiated in the brighter hallway above the deputy's head. The old man studied him, noting the scuffed boots and the khakis loosely hanging on a frame of prominent and elongate bones, the circles beneath his eyes. The lean and hungry look of him.

He said, "Your two compadres have kind of a brisk manner about them." Millimaki sat with his hands clasped, forearms resting on his thighs. He smiled at the floor between his feet but the old man could not see his face and he went on. "You seemed to be the odd man out in that dog and pony show." Again, Millimaki merely sat. He turned one wrist slightly to consult his watch. Finally the old man leaned from his chair, one eye squinted against the unaccustomed light or the smoke from the cigarette in the corner of his mouth to read the nametag on the young deputy's shirtfront. "That's a mouthful. What is it, Finn or something?"

"Yeah, Finn," Millimaki said. "I didn't have any say in the matter. The other half is Bohunk."

Gload smoked. "Hell of a deal." He held a bean can bent to accept a cigarette in its edge and he tipped his ash into it. "I knew a lot of Finlanders and Hunkies down in Butte. A lot of 'em. Micks, too. You take the Harps and Finns and Bohunks out of Butte and you got a couple of Wops and a Welshman standing around a hole in the ground with their dicks in their hands."

Millimaki said, "I'll have to take your word for it."

"Well," the old man said, "that's how it was."

By shift's end the old man was back in his cell, thoughtful and quietly smoking, and Millimaki left him and the jail and drove toward the grassy dune country southwest out of town where above the languid horseshoe bends of the Missouri River a settlement in recent years had sprung up, outsized homes he'd heard the sheriff once call "monuments to power

and wealth." On the sandy bluff the surgeon's house where he
was to meet his wife appeared fortresslike against the dusk, its
roofline a complex topography of hips and gables and Dutch
hip dormers and a phallic tower with a dome of hammered
copper which at that hour beaconed its russet affluence to
the working-class homes on the river below. From the hilltop
eminence the prefabs and double-wide trailers looked like
shoe boxes or children's blocks set haphazardly beside a papier-
mâché stream. The department made calls with equal frequency
to the homes of the wealthy for spousal abuse and ODed teens
and skeletal anorexic wives on the roadway in their teddies
strung out and waving handguns at the passing cars. Millimaki
had discovered fairly quickly that the problems of the rich were
much the same as those of the unrich, though in the savage
glare of the booking-room lights their sportswear and excellent
dental work made for more attractive photographs.

What he could see of the yard sloped down to the water's
edge, the acreage neatly cordoned from the rampant weeds of
the vacant adjacent lots by a welded pole fence of black metal. In
the center of the yard a bosk of sculpted junipers in the descending twilight looked like mourners nodding above a grave. A single robin sat atop the fence, a bold brushstroke of color, its breast
more sanguine for the backdrop of freakish April snow.

At the sheltered entry, a black iron footman greeted Millimaki and tendered his servitude with an upraised tray and a
rictus of gleaming teeth. The woman who answered his knock
affected a wide-eyed look of theatrical fear.

"Oh, Gawd," she said. "You finally caught up with me." She
threw her hands up, a cocktail the color of emeralds bleeding
down her arm, a dozen thin silver bracelets chiming.

Millimaki forced a smile. "My wife is here," he said. The woman went away howling. He found Glenda in an enormous room standing among several men and she managed a quick kiss on his cheek.

Their host called it the great room and from its twelve-foot walls glassine eyes of exotic trophy heads regarded the guests, well-turned-out men and women already aglow and garrulous from drink. Though it was barely spring and there was snow on the ground, a few of the men wore no socks with their tasseled loafers. They were polite. Millimaki sensed as they gripped his hand they were formulating a diagnosis from the dull thrum of his pulse, the red of his eye.

He wandered beneath the gaudy taxidermy and stood finally before a bank of windows watching the evening dim and the great room lights appear as uncertain phosphorescent portals on the black water below. A nurse whom Millimaki had always thought of as an older and heavier version of his wife swept toward him and gave him an uncomfortably long hug.

"Howdy, Sheriff. Come to arrest me?"

"I sort of heard that one already tonight, Jean."

"Oh, shit. I hate being unoriginal."

"That's all right. Yours came with more warmth."

She put her hand on his arm. "Are you okay? Your eyes look like two piss holes in a snowbank."

"Now that's better. That's fresh stuff."

"I mean it."

"I'm fine, Jean."

His wife was across the room, cornered by a man who seemed to be indicating where an incision might be made on her chest. Jean glanced their way and squeezed Millimaki's arm.

"What can I get you to drink, Val?"

"I think Glenda has a head start so I'll have to drive us home."

"She's staying with me tonight, didn't she tell you?"

Above his wife and her companion a leopard was poised to leap from stagecraft cover of savannah grass, its jaundiced eyes bright as candle flames beneath the floodlights.

"Of course. Right," he said.

"I'll just get one more for myself and that's it." Jean moved off somewhat unsteadily toward a table arrayed with bottles and containers of ice. At the same time a Japanese woman who worked with his wife in the ICU approached from the makeshift bar. She had been married to an Air Force major and they'd lived on the base east of the town, a sprawling city-state of tarmac and austere cinder-block buildings where the green of lawns and trees after the brief springtimes faded quickly to the color of the prairie and the window glass in the identical houses shuddered under the bellowing of lumbering cargo jets and where she one day awoke to find the major gone. The surprise of her abandonment never left her face and when she bore down on Millimaki her eyes were wide and her tiny mouth was set in an O. She chattered excitedly about his debt book. Her voice was shrill and her accent thick and he was not sure what she'd said.

"I'm sorry. My what?"

"Debt book, debt book." She pantomimed with frantic fluttering hands the turning of pages. "Book. With all your debt people in it."

"I'm not getting—"

Jean had come with her drink and put her hand on his forearm. "She means 'dead,' Val."

"Yes, debt, of course. With collecting pictures of debt people. How funny."

He began to explain that he took the pictures as part of his work, but she was already reeling off toward a group of men clustered beneath the grizzled head of a Cape buffalo, the great sweep of its horns under the floodlights glowing like burnished ebony. "How funny," he could hear her say. "Debt pictures of debt people." Her voice from across the cavernous room sounded like breaking glass. The men looked at her and as she pointed looked at Millimaki.

Jean said, "I'm sorry, Val. Let's call it a cultural thing."

"Did Glenda tell you guys about those pictures?"

"No, Val. I'm sure she wouldn't have done that."

But she must have said something, he thought. Dead book. Had Glenda called it that? But debt book, that was also true. He did owe something to the dead.

The woman from the front door swept by and spoke without stopping or looking at him. "I'm a goddamn fugitive from justice." She was shoeless, her dress iridescent.

"Somebody's having a good time."

"She's harmless," Jean said. Millimaki saw her across the room. She eyed him malignly from over the rim of her neon tumbler. Her virid tongue flicked like a lizard's.

Like a jackal harmless, he thought. She should be skulking through the veldt among the other predators on the great room's wall.

They drove down the long slope of the hill with the house blazing behind them, and soon were on the river flats. In silence they passed shabby shotgun houses and tire-buttressed trailers where no window lights burned and the river rolled beside the road like oil, in the headlights cannibalized pickups set on blocks, appliances upended and rusting, the acetylene eyes of feral cats.

In the sudden lights of town the traffic was sparse and she directed him wordlessly to the apartment complex. He parked the truck beneath the polar glow of halogens and left the engine idling. The wind shook the lamp poles and the truck shuddered in the gusts. Low gray berms of plowed snow seemed animated under the quaking light.

Millimaki said, "I guess I'd better get going. Tom will be pissing and moaning like I haven't fed him for a month. He'll make me feel like a bad person."

"He'll be fine."

The apartment building was a bleak three-level box, one of several adjacent to the hospital. Everything about was asphalt, everything weirdly pale beneath the wobbling arc lights.

Millimaki said, "At what point were you going to tell me you were staying in town?"

"Well, I thought I did. Didn't I? You can see it makes sense." She extended her wrist toward the dashlight glow to see the watch dial. "I have to be at work in six hours."

"Yeah. It makes sense. I just wish I didn't have to hear it from Jean and look like an ass."

"Jean loves you. You couldn't look like an ass to her. She has a thing for you."

"She's a nice lady. I don't get that kind of take on the rest of the crowd."

She sat rigidly, gloved hands in her lap. "Those are my friends and colleagues."

"Yes, and by the way, did you catch your colleague's slave décor by the front door?"

"Of all the wonderful things in that house, that's all you can comment on?"

"I didn't notice any other racist appointments. He may have had some."

"It's not a slave just because it's black, Val. It's an antique."

"Well, just because it's old doesn't make it not a nigger waiting to hitch up Massa's Beamer after a long day in the OR."

"Oh, for God's sake." She stared into the windshield. The truck's heater fan whirred. After a long while she said dreamily, "It's a beautiful lovely house. I mean everything is so—"

"Everything is so bought."

She didn't turn to look at him. Whatever she saw in the dark glass still held her. "You could have tried, Val," she said at last.

"They were trying. They are talented intelligent men."

"Glenda, when I'm expending all of my energy trying not to punch someone in the throat for staring at my wife's ass."

"That's ridiculous."

"I have eyes."

"Yes," she said. "You have cop eyes."

"Cop eyes?" he said. He turned on the seat to look at her. "This is new."

"Just the way you look at things. Eyes that see around corners and under things where nobody else would think to look."

He felt the night's tension begin to veer toward a novel savagery. Unconsciously he dug one hand into the seat as if he might hold them in place against the quickening current. His long exhalation fogged the window glass.

"Okay," he said. "Look, it's just that I don't have a thing in common with those guys."

"You could have talked about hunting. You could have talked about that."

"A goddamn rhino, Glenda. There was not one head shot in this country. Hell, on this continent."

"Well. It's still hunting."

"It is and it isn't. I mean a Chevy's a car and a, whatever, a Lamborghini's a car. The same, in name only."

"But you know what, Val? When I'm with your sheriff's department Neanderthals I try."

"Once. Exactly one party you came to with me."

"That's not true."

"One time. In three and a half years. And 'Neanderthals'?"

"That's not fair, of course. The sheriff seems very nice. One or two others I remember with eyebrows that didn't meet in the middle."

They sat staring out at the desolate lot. Trash cartwheeled past and caught up against cars parked in their numbered spaces. From a gap in a hedge of half-dead arborvitae a lean brindle dog shot past trailing a tether, its hair roached up on its back by the wind and it trotted with its head oddly angled to avoid stepping on the rope. In the harsh odd light its ribs showed clearly. She watched it until it vanished into the gloom between the austere complexes. Overhead powerlines swayed perilously, their shadows writhing on the icy pavement. When she spoke again her voice had softened.

"If the wind would not blow for one day."

"You'll wish a long time for that."

She moved her slender wrist again into the green dashboard light.

"I guess I'd better go in before Jean locks me out."

"Does she have an extra bed?"

"A couch. A foldout."

"That's just torture," he said. "Does she have rocks? Rocks would be more comfortable."

"I'll be fine for one night." She reached over and patted his hand briefly where it lay between them on the seat. "You be careful driving home."

"I will."

They both got out of the truck into the raw nighttime and she ran for the shelter of a stairwell. He stood there for a moment with the wind rifling down his jacket and whipping his pants legs and watched until he saw her on the second-level walkway hurrying beneath weak amber bulbs. She stopped at a door without looking back and disappeared within.

He considered the hour drive to the empty house in the hills where the snow would still be ankle deep. "That's all right," he said. "You can kiss me twice tomorrow night." He got behind the wheel and looked up at the apartment door. "Or a wave. That might have been nice."

During the first week of the trial, the young deputy took John Gload from his cell to the courthouse and escorted him to chambers to meet with his lawyer and he walked with him to the bathroom and during noon recess carried his lunch to him in the holding area. At the dark end of the day he held Gload's elbow like an old companion as they crossed the frozen courthouse yard on the icy sidewalks, the old man in his leg irons shuffling among the stark shadows of still-leafless elms as black as columns of anthracite in the pearl moonlight of early April.

Gload said little during this time to anyone, and Millimaki made no attempt to draw him out. What conversation there was was remote and quotidian, the kind any two strangers might exchange. A word about the food, the weather. For the most part the old man sat before the high bench in the courtroom beside his lawyer with his head erect and unmoving and with his enormous arms atop the table in the pose of a leonine statue. Occasionally he slid a yellow legal pad close and scribbled on it feverishly. At times Millimaki caught the old man looking at him appraisingly where he stood nearby. When Millimaki returned his stare he did not look away and he did not smile.

When the week was out, on a Monday, Weldon Wexler assumed Millimaki's escort duties and would take the old man to and from the courtroom where the nature or duration of his life would be decided. He'd been with the department a year longer than Millimaki and had parlayed this seniority and a troubling knee into a request for light duty, relegating Millimaki to an indefinite period of night shift at the jail. When they passed in the corridor that morning Wexler favored him with a smirk and a short two-fingered salute. He limped away down the bright corridor, favoring first one knee then the other, hair freshly barbered and meticulously combed, his uniform trousers creased smartly, sharp creases beneath the pockets of his shirt. Buckles, buttons, the snaps on his holster, polished to the luster of servingware. The men in their cells who like feral dogs sensed weakness in any form mocked him in hushed tones and would in the deep witnessless hours of the night concoct from his slewing gait and pretty mouth salacious tableaus, hissed from cage to cage to cage like some lascivious burlesque.

Valentine Millimaki would not see John Gload in the light of day for a month and his own wife for nearly as long. He left his small house in the foothills of the Little Belt Mountains as

the sun burned to an ember through the timber at the ridgetops
even as his wife arrived home and he spent the long nights
ambling listlessly about the old building or sitting outside the
prisoners' cells, nearly maddened with boredom and claustro-
phobia.

He found it almost impossible to adapt to this place where
in enduring his eight- or ten-hour shift he would differ so little
from his charges in their cages.

All but asleep on his feet at the jailer's desk on the third
night, he was roused by the appearance through the streetside
door of Voyle Dobek and another veteran deputy and they carried between them a slight dark figure seemingly as boneless as
a straw man, the toes of his shoes squealing as he was dragged
roughly along the polished floor. They turned toward the
sally gate, blowing and sweating like draft horses and when
Millimaki came forward Dobek said, "Just stick your ass right
there, Millimaki, and buzz us in. We'll take care of this blan-
ketass."

When he saw the man next, at three-thirty in the morning,
he was shivering violently. The sound of his teeth chattering
brought Val to the bars and he saw the man sitting on the bunk
with the rough wool issue blanket wrapped around him and
cowled monklike over his head. The hand that held the blanket
was overlarge for a man his size, abraded and deeply fissured.

Millimaki said, "Are you sick?"

He was a Cree from the Rocky Boy reservation, his face in
the beam of Millimaki's flashlight a death's-head of sunken
cheeks and eyes in their caves the color of coal.

The man could barely speak. "Them bastards held me down
in a g-goddamn puddle and I can't can't can't get warmed up no
more."

Millimaki reached through the bars and felt the sleeve of the man's worn western shirt. "You're soaked."

"I'm all s-soakin' wet and I can't get warm."

"I'll get you something."

He had a spare shirt in his truck and he came with that and another blanket and a cup of burned coffee from the office hot plate. He'd expected to smell liquor when he entered the cell but he did not. The small man shook so badly he could not negotiate the shirt's buttons and the deputy was forced to do it for him.

"All's I wanted to do was to talk to her. That was all. I never in my life put a hand on that woman. She's a drunk. I'm worried about my kids."

"Yeah," Millimaki said. "Okay."

"She's taken up with some white dude. I think he might be some kind of meth-head or something. Some junkie. I come down after work and all's I want to do is to talk to her, man. Now I'm fixing to lose my job."

"Where do you work?"

"I bust tires at a place up in Big Sandy. I ain't never missed a day in four and some years."

Millimaki took out his notebook and pen. "Write down the name of the place and your boss." The little man wrote, his knobbly hand working laboriously across the small page, shaking.

"I don't know that you can read that. See if you can."

Millimaki read it back and the man said it was right.

"What's your name?"

"George Gopher. Georgie they call me."

"Drink that coffee."

"I ain't drunk, you know. Them sonsofbitches said I was drunk but I ain't."

"I know you're not. Just to warm you up is what I meant."

"All right." He sipped at the cup, made a face. He held up one arm and the shirtsleeve dangled over his hand. "This shirt's too big for me."

"So sue me. I forgot your size."

"It's all right."

When he left George Gopher's cell half an hour later, the man was asleep on his cot under the two blankets and the hallway was as quiet as a mortuary. One of the tube lights was failing and it strobed weirdly, his footfalls syncopated like an antique movie reel and into this light a plume of cigarette smoke bloomed from John Gload's cell.

The long hallway with its cells had been painted yellow halfway up and it looked as though it had, a half century before, endured a flood of bile. On one of the first nights Millimaki walked down, his boot heels resounded hollowly and above the insect-burr of the tubelights and from the invisible interiors of the cells came the sounds of sleeping men and their smells—sweat and hair cream, aftershave, urine, from some a distinctive metallic smell that Millimaki had decided was the smell of fear.

The thin Cree Georgie Gopher had made bail and was back north earning his difficult living and bearing upon those narrow shoulders the great burden of his endangered children.

Millimaki paused at the end of the hall, cocking his ear at a noise that might have been someone strangling, but it was only snoring or a man in that aphotic place struggling against some malign hands in dream. He was about to turn when a voice said, "Seems you got the shit-end of some stick or other, Deptee."

"You scared the shit out of me, John. I thought everybody was asleep."

"Sleep," the old man said wistfully. "I don't sleep much, kid."

Millimaki approached the cell door and in the slant of light could make out but Gload's disembodied legs and huge hands and wrists. The hands disappeared momentarily and he heard a scritch and then the flare of the match and Gload's visage appeared for an instant from the black like a mask passed before a stage light.

"What's the deal with this Weldon asshole?"

"Deputy Wexler, I think you mean."

"Yeah, Wexler. Sorry-ass little turd. He wants me to call him Weldon I guess so we can be pals." He grunted. "What'd you do to miss out on baby-sitting me, anyways? Seems like pretty fair duty."

"Deputy Wexler has seniority on me. And he's nursing a bum knee."

Gload snorted. A pale cloud formed from out of the dark of his cell. "Right. From chasing bad guys." He seemed incredulous. "That's what he honest to Christ said." He waited for Millimaki to say something but he did not. "Seems to get around on that war wound pretty good unless somebody's watching him." He snorted again. Millimaki would come to understand in the coming weeks that this was what passed for a laugh from the old man.

"I don't know anything about how he got it."

"He tells me you're a farm kid. But he kind of says it like he has a mouthful of shit."

He knew Gload was fishing, whether to combat the boredom of stir or for some other reason, and he chose to ignore it. He had been around enough of these jailbirds to know that it was

mesh of gear on gear marking the order of time. He closed his eyes. But in a short time he realized that the gulls that night were particularly active, swarming behind his eyelids in a maelstrom of soiled feathers and beaks stained with gore. So he lay in the plot of darkness now allotted him in the world thinking about the woman who waited for him at home.

THREE

The morning following the night on the dam they drove east six hours to Rapid City to exchange for currency what they had earned from their labors: a trunkload of antique glassware. The young gay man they had kidnapped and murdered had inherited much of the collection and had added to it over a decade, never dreaming the seashell plates and fluted glasses so lovingly arrayed about his dead mother's house where he lived yet would be the vehicles of his own death.

They drove the bright spring day in near total silence, the kid sleepy and still pouting from Gload having stuck a gun in his ear and the cold and quiet atmosphere suited the old man.

In Roundup they stopped to eat and the kid, revitalized at the prospect of food, flirted with the waitress. She was a girl of nineteen or twenty and White stared after her stout bare legs as she walked away.

He said, "How'd you like to have those clamped around yer ass?" Gload looked up from his paper briefly and looked back. "She'd about buck you off and that's no shit," the kid said.

When the girl came back with their platters, Sid looked up at her. Above her left breast was a tag with the name Jessy laboriously printed in childish block letters.

"Jessy," Sid said. "Hey, now, what's the name of the other one?" The girl set the plates down and looked over her shoulder.

"I'm the only one on today," she said. She smiled down at him, a pretty girl twenty pounds overweight with gaps in her teeth and sorrel hair in a knot atop her head, the seams and buttons on her uniform restraining burgeoning excesses of soft flesh at hip and bosom.

Sid shook his head. "No, the other one." He pointed at her tag, at her breast. She shook her head in confusion. "Hell, your other tittie," he said. "This here one's named Jessy, I can see that, but you ain't named the other one."

Gload looked up at the girl briefly and then at White. "Shut your mouth," he said. He spun his plate of eggs and ham around in front of him on the newspaper and began eating and those were the last words spoken between them until they reached Rapid City three and a half hours later.

The building was weathered board and bat, proclaiming in great red letters on its façade: "Old West Trading Post." The duckboards leading to saloon doors lay in a piebald shade beneath an archway of woven antlers. A marquee atop an iron pole of rudely welded four-inch pipe rose from within a ring of whitewashed stones, bearing skyward its message: "Coldest Beer in the west, postcards, IndiaN beAdwork, friendly. Clean rooms afFordable. Genuine antiquEs of the OLd West."

Gload pointed wordlessly and Sid nosed the big car up to a

hitching rail. He swung the door open and said, "Stay in the car."

"We're partners on this deal," Sid said.

Gload, standing outside the car, leaned his head down to speak into the open door.

"Stay in the fucking car."

In ten minutes he came back. White sat brooding with his boots propped on the car's dash, his arms crossed at his chest.

Gload said, "Get your feet off of there. We'll meet the man tonight, eight o'clock. Drive around to the side over here." He fumbled with the plastic key fob. "One oh one." He glared at the swinging doors and at the name in foot-high gold letters above them. "Colonel," he said. He spat onto the gravel between his feet. "What's he a fucking colonel of?"

"I don't know."

"Colonel of bullshit, maybe."

"What'd he say?"

Gload went to the passenger side door and got in. "One oh one," he said. He pointed with the key. "Over there."

"Don't I even get my own room?"

"Once we take care of business you can get you a room and stay a month for all I give a shit," Gload said. "Until then we stay together." He looked over at him. "Partner."

Full dark at that early hour afforded them cover to unload from the car's trunk the boxes of plates and cups and saucers, glasses, glazed and painted bowls and all manner of dishware, the uses for which Gload could only guess. He had no more interest in them than in stones or books or the workings of a car's engine. He was in many ways as simple as a child, though without a child's curiosity. In the efficiency of his work he took pride though not necessarily pleasure, any more than would a man running sawlogs through a mill or for his prescribed hours soldering senseless components onto a board. He was handy at his work and it afforded him a living. His pleasures were few and modest—sitting in the sun at the door of his house in the orchard above the Breaks; a slow drive along the vacant county gravel roads with Francie to park finally above the river to watch the sun fall down toward the crimson close of the day. Once a year he loaded a stout pole and reel and drug the muddy Missouri bottom for paddlefish.

The Colonel, a small wizened figure seeming smaller yet within his huge swivel chair, instructed Sid the Kid to display the goods on a long folding table, making benevolent sweeping motions as he spoke and when this was done he got up with pipe in hand and walked up and down before them as if inspecting troops, picking up an occasional saucer or bowl to squint at runes on its underside. Gload had taken a chair opposite the Colonel and the exhibited wares, that he might see the man's eyes. He smoked and appeared to pay little attention to the production. Like a tradesman, his talents were primarily manual—the use of a knife, manipulation of flesh—but they ran also to cards and the reading of men's faces. So when the Colonel sat back and packed his pipe and said a number, Gload stubbed out his cigarette, stood and walked through the door into the night without a word, as though he were taken with a mild whim or notion, or had remembered suddenly some domestic errand. The Colonel and Sid White sat quietly dandling their feet in their chairs. They did so for fifteen minutes. The Colonel began to swivel and fidget in his chair and Sid began to sweat.

As if to answer a question that had not been asked, Sid said, "Well, hell, I don't know. He might of had, you know, one of

them deals." He made a rotating motion near his ear. "A stroke."
He rose. "I'd best go and check on him."

As he left the room the little man said, "It's a generous offer,
tell him. A handsome offer."

Gload sat in the room, smoking. He had turned on the TV
but did not seem engaged by it. He sat with his head leaned back
on the chair watching the smoke curl up to the ceiling. He had
put his slippers on.

Sid looked at him incredulously. "What're you doing? He's
waiting back there."

Gload smoked. Presently he spoke, very slowly, as if instruct-
ing a child. "How much did the kid who previously owned all
that shit say it was worth?" He continued to study the smoke,
White presented with a view of the bristled hollows of the older
man's throat.

"What he said might not of been right," White said. "He
might of just been a fag trying to be Mister Big Shot."

Gload only sat, waiting, his head back. One slippered foot
jounced up and down to some slow rhythm sounding in his head.

"Okay," Sid said, "he said seventeen-five."

"Seventeen-five," Gload repeated. "And your new buddy over
there, the Colonel, offered what was it again?"

"It's a handsome offer."

Gload's eyes were small and black like a pig's and when he
dropped his head and turned them on the kid, in the fluxing
television glow they flashed a brief radioactive spark.

"Okay, okay," the kid said. "Eight thousand dollars. That's a
shitload of money for dishes."

"Eight thousand dollars. A difference of what?"

Sid sat figuring for some time. He began to cast about for
pencil and paper.

Gload said, "Nine thousand five hundred dollars."

"Right. Nine-five."

Gload held a single finger aloft as if to admonish White to listen to something outside the room. White looked about, his head canted.

"What?" he said.

"That," said Gload. "The sound of the Colonel making money off other people's sweat and travail."

White stood helplessly, his hands outstretched in an attitude of supplication.

"Travail?"

"My sweat and travail."

The kid said, "Well, what do I tell him?" A vision he'd begun to concoct of himself attired in a western-cut Porter Waggoner–style suit, its trouser pockets ballasted with folded bills in a begemmed clip, began to wobble and fade. Even half of the money the Colonel had offered was money beyond reckoning. He had worked washing dishes in an Italian restaurant in Black Eagle and he had sold batteries stolen from cars and he had once worked briefly as a hay hand in the Judith Basin, feigning heat sickness after one long hot morning atop a haystack, riding to town on the bus and licking his blistered palms like a dog. From that foray into ranch work Sid White considered himself a cowboy. Four thousand dollars was the stuff of hallucination. "He ain't going to sit there and wait on us forever."

"With an offer of what he said he can sit and wait till doomsday comes," Gload said. "If you come back here without a number in your mouth that is twelve thousand then I am gone home. And I'll not send you back with a different number. I'll not dicker like a Mexican over a clay pot. There is one number that will work and I just told you it."

Sid White stood openmouthed in front of Gload, who had
by then turned to the television and begun roaming the sta-
tions, his face no more than a foot from the screen as he turned
the dial, its crags awash in a kaleidoscope of lurid colors. This
old man, White thought, is going to get me fucked over. He
considered his options and decided that should the numbers
not work he could come back with something in his pocket to
take care of John Gload. Gload was an old man and the kid
didn't care about all the things he had supposedly done a hundred years ago. He wastes one queer, so what? He would still
go down with a blade in his spine, same as any man would. He
could make a deal with the Colonel, he was sure, and who
would miss this sonofabitch with anyway one foot already in
the grave?

"We could go ten," the kid said. "Show our good whatcha-
call. Intentions."

"I am leaving in the morning with what I said or nothing,"
Gload said to the television screen. "And the shit goes back in
the trunk."

In ten minutes the kid came into the room and sat on the
edge of one of the beds. Gload did not look up. White sat with
his hands on his knees, his mouth slightly ajar. He sat so for
some time, his tongue darting out with the regularity of a heart-
beat. Finally he said, "Well, I will be goddamned all to hell." He
looked at Gload then. "He said come in in the morning and he'll
have the money." The kid was looking at Gload's great sloping
back beneath a T-shirt worn to near transparency. A gray fringe
of hair bristled at the neck. "Hey, old man, I said he'll have the
money. What you wanted, twelve grand, all of it." He shook his
head. "He didn't piss and moan or nothing. Just sat there for a
half minute and said it: come by in the morning. Unfucking-

believable." He was about to clap the old man on the back, but thought better of it.

"You are something else, you know that?"

Gload looked up then. He said, "You left the door open."

Morning, heralded by a raw wind that pawed and moaned at the door and by a bar of wan light beneath the draperies, saw John Gload paring his nails in the coned light of a bed lamp and on the twin bed opposite Sidney White was an inappreciable bundle, as though beneath the horse blanket bedspread stickwood and stones were arranged to approximate the shape of a man. A faint whistle issued from under the covers and on the pillow Gload could see but the top of the boy's head, a medusa of lank blue-black stringlets against the linen. He sat with the knife in his hand for a long time.

An hour later White sat in the passenger seat of the car, bleary-eyed and shivering in his thin denim jacket, and watched as Gload came from the Colonel's office, slewing bearlike down the ludicrous duckboard walkway. The car was loaded and running and John Gload settled behind the wheel. From an envelope he counted out ten five hundred dollar notes and handed them across to the kid.

"This ain't half," White said. "I can figure that much."

Gload levered the car in gear and pulled onto the highway west, the asphalt a ribbon of brass unspooling in the rearview mirror, wherein small birds feeding at the road edge rose like sea spume and tumbled shimmering in their slipstream.

"You were ready to settle for four and you get five," Gload said. "What you might call a 'handsome offer.'"

The kid regarded Gload's profile, adamantine as those granite visages chiseled from the mountain a few miles' drive south.

He fanned the money in his hands—new stiff bills, undreamed-of fortune—and knew it was pointless to argue. As they sped past the array of strip malls and truck stops, he sat with his forehead against the side window. He said, "What a fucked-up town."

By the time they got to Miles City the kid's mood had brightened considerably. His head swiveled as they drove through town and he took note of the number of bars and of the garish rodeo posters in shop fronts of bucking and rearing horses and he goggled at teenage girls with books clamped to their chests and their long hair swaying down their backs. Suddenly he turned to Gload and said, "What's the best hotel in this shithole?"

"Pioneer, I suppose. Used to be anyway."

"Drop me off there."

"It was on the other end of town. We passed it."

The kid seemed not to hear. He sat with his face pressed to the window glass, patting his left breast pocket wherein the folded bills lay, and Gload shook his head. It would not be long, he knew, before the kid and money parted company. He slowed and glanced at his mirrors and U-turned the car in the wide avenue, cranking the wheel around with one finger.

"If I can't get laid here," the kid said, "I don't have a hair on my ass."

Having retrieved his small gym bag from the trunk, the kid swung open the passenger side door and leaning in made a gun of his thumb and forefinger, aimed it at the old man behind the wheel. He said, "Okay. I'll catch you back on the home turf, pardner." Gload bent down to watch him mount the hotel steps, swaggering atop three-inch riding heels with his jeans stuffed bronc rider style into his boot tops. He paused at the door to

rake back his snarled hair and turn up his collar and he swept
into the lobby like some kind of outland prince come to take
the little town by storm. For all that, Gload thought, he was no
more than a boy.

Some time later he stopped the car at a small creek which
like an oasis in the bald prairieland along its course supported a
stand of old cottonwoods. He walked through the tangled ditch
weeds into the trees, the trunks gray and immense as menhirs.
An incongruous crane labored up from the bracken along the
muddy stream, towing its lean shadow through the heeling bluestem toward water rumored in the distance by a slash of green.
Gload stood and relieved his swollen bladder against a tree and
stared up into branches so high the ragged April scud seemed
caught there like wisps of tapestry, a high circling bird caged in a
wickerwork of pale spring bud. He stood for a long while, until
the earth under his feet became as capricious as the deck of a
ship. The line of song in his head was this, from when or where
he could not remember: "Above Earth's Lamentation."

FOUR

They'd come for Gload in the late afternoon. He'd had time to put things in careful order and he sat for perhaps the last time on his chair, listening to the calls and flutterings of birds just arrived north and looking at the desolate faces of last year's sunflowers at the orchard's verge. He felt strangely at peace. He got up once and walked down the little orchard lane, bordered already by senseless weeds woven like basketry and he stared long across the sage where the river was. He kept his eyes there as he walked and soon they appeared, like wind-borne trash, rising and falling from view and appearing again, kiting effortlessly on set wings. The old man felt their terrible eyes on him.

The wind shook the trees and their branches gnashed and shuddered and the wheat-pale needlegrass down every row lay on the ground. He stood at the prescribed spot looking through the gnarled trunks beyond which the sun burned slowly down. He moved forward a few paces and looked and he moved back, trying to see it as a stranger might. He squinted his eyes and through the ruddled apertures the cured orchard grass and the dark slender tree boles quaking against the sky were an impressionist's blur of blue, ocher, dun. The grass bowed and hissed in the wind and waiting he heard the dull pong of the harrow tines, hung in a tree like a rude mobile or wind chime, and then he went back.

Long before they arrived he could see the dust trail, patrol cars dragging a dirty cumulus across the evening sky, and he could see within it lights throbbing like a foundry fire and finally the cars themselves appeared, bumping and slewing up the narrow road, their windshields aflame.

They found a house in neat order, dishes washed, bed made, plants in pots set up to the south-facing windows newly watered. They found Francie's clothes and perfumes and creams, her shoes paired and aligned in a closet. They asked about her and John Gload told them she was gone and he did not lie.

Five weeks later, astride the chair in his cell, John Gload recalled the moment under the cottonwood trees, not as one of the greatest miscalculations of his career but the instant of its realization. Standing pissing on a tree and embarked upon one course of action, the other concocting itself like a visitation out of the leaves of the trees.

That morning Sid White had been led shuffling into the courtroom and he wasn't in such spirits as Gload had seen him last. He sat hunched and childlike in a strange purple suit piped in gold and around his gaping shirt collar a bolo tie cinched with an outlandish shard of turquoise. Entering he did not raise a hand in greeting or so much as meet the old man's eyes, as he seemed altogether transfixed by the troubling new jewelry adorning his wrists and ankles.

Out of the cell's tangible dark Gload alchemized an early morning in Rapid City. He sat beneath yellow lamplight with the knife in his hand as the kid slept and it would have been such an easy thing, a simple matter of drawing back the coverlet, getting a grip of hair and pulling the blade across Sid White's throat. For that matter, he could have gotten in the car, driven back from the grove of cottonwoods a scant hundred miles and waited in the room in Miles City for the kid to come back drunk. In a way, he thought, it was like two mistakes, one stacked on top of the other. "I could of had him rolled in a bed quilt, into the trunk and underground and it wouldn't of cost me no more than two hours tops," he said.

As he spoke, the young deputy who had befriended him came to sit in his accustomed chair. Millimaki thought with the appearance of Sid White today that the old man would be inclined to talk. He seemed, though, to regard Millimaki as no more animate than the chair he occupied. Gload sat back and disappeared into the darkness and a match flame revealed a ghostly theatrical mask of profound abstraction.

Millimaki said, "Did you say something, John?"

The old killer said, "For example, there's one thing that if I would of done it and if I would of followed my goddamn instinks I'd be sitting in my little trees right now with a blanket on my lap. Instead." He raised his hands palm up, turning his head left and right, inviting the attendant darkness to regard the conditions of his current life.

Val turned in his chair to see if perhaps someone had come silently to stand behind him.

Gload sat astraddle his chair, his hands atop his knees and his chin nearly on his chest. He looked very old then, his thin gray hair awry and hanging before his eyes and Val could see deep vertical creases in his neck like watercourses.

"What one thing, John?"

Gload shook his head ruefully.

"The trouble with being old in my business is that all your old partners are dead or laying up dying slow in the joint somewheres. I was plumb out of good help, is how I come to get White. The young blood," he said wearily. "Good Lord." A hand rose from his knee as if of its own accord and he sat looking at the burning cigarette there and then put it to his lips. He spoke squinting through the smoke. "I tried to show him some things, but the way it is with these young guys is they already know everything and they want to be the boss. If they don't know shit from apple butter." A pause, a long liquid exhale from the shadows. "Golf clubs," he said. "Sweet Jesus."

"What? Golf clubs? Are you talking about Sid White?"

Gload continued. Millimaki felt invisible. "There's times when you do that—look back and think, I should of done this or that or some other thing. Like with that kid. I don't have a lot of those times, a handful, but what I do know is that you can't never ever let them get under your skin. You did what you did at the time and at the time it was right. I regret almost nothing. This thing here lately. Some others. But I ain't been eat up by them, either."

Val consulted his watch and waited. The night was well advanced. The old man sighed and Millimaki thought he might continue but he withdrew without a word and from the darkness came the creak of bunk chains.

Val sat for a moment longer and stood to leave. From the dark came Gload's voice. "Television. That's the problem," he said. "They seen it all on the television."

FIVE

When Millimaki pulled into the yard the rancher who had phoned in the plate numbers stood leaning against a porch post, at four in the afternoon red-eyed and holding a tumbler a third full of something that looked like tea but was not. He did little more than point with his glass hand toward the low ridge where the car was and seemed otherwise indisposed to talk. Two scabrous heelers came on a dead run from a hay barn that leaned from its footings six inches from plumb and they made immediately for the flanks of the tracking dog and Val was forced to kick at them. When he turned the man had gone in, and when he came down off the mountain four hours later in the semidark there was no light burning anywhere on the place.

It was a seldom-used ranch road the missing old man had taken, an apparently random turn from a random highway at the end of a fuddled and reckless drive. He had laid down the right-of-way gate and driven over the gate wires and posts and in the old Buick had bucked and churned upslope until the tires sank axle deep in the mud of a seep-spring.

On the floorboards of the LeSabre were newspapers and balled filthy clothing and the dog snuffled at them, looking at Millimaki with his sad wet eyes and then set out lunging at his lead with the scent in his nose. The road wound steeply upward through sparse dwarf pine lopsided and scoured by the vicious winds that inhabited that place and then along a ridgetop where rocky spines like the backs of antediluvian plated beasts protruded from the soil. The wind did blow and it moaned among the trees and the dirt from the bare ridge seethed in the grass as the dog surged ahead, whining. Below and ahead of them an ancient tree rose from the center of a great rock, its limbs accoutered with crows. As man and dog approached, the birds rose by twos and threes croaking, their black beaks agape like panting dogs', and their ragged wings beat furiously to hold against the wind.

He had apparently tripped or had suffered a seizure or heart attack on the ridge and then had fallen head over heels like a circus tumbler, becoming lodged head downhill in the split trunk of the tree the birds had occupied. Old sawyers called these trees schoolmarms and the man's head was wedged in the V of the trunk and was enlarged and black as a chunk of coal. His footfalls soundless through the pine duff, Millimaki circled the tree slowly, the film in the 35mm advancing with a whirr. He photographed close-up the terrible thing and then with some effort pried it from its horrible cunnilingual embrace and laid it back, where it sat rigored on the sidehill like a charred gargoyle. The dog sat whimpering. Millimaki snapped more pictures of the troll-like thing balanced on the slope and finally for his own purposes photographed the tree itself, groping freakishly into the daylight and wind as if from a stone egg, with its complement of funereal birds returned raucously to claim their rightful place.

The mountains there were beyond the truck radio's range and by the time he roused the rancher to call the coroner for permission to remove the body it was near dark. The rancher sat nearby at his kitchen table listening, dressed in the coveralls he had slept in. Millimaki negotiated the use of an ATV and a small cart. The exchange took perhaps ten words. The vehicle's headlight when he arrived once again on the mountain pulsed bright and dim apace with its ragged idling and in this weird light he bagged the awkward corpse and rolled it onto the haycart among fencing pliers and staples and metal posts and at his truck loaded it with difficulty into the bed like a bale of wet hay.

By the time he exchanged vehicles and made the drive to town through the dark on the empty highway and delivered his package to the morgue it was nearly six o'clock, and when he at last got home his wife was gone to work and his bed without her in it seemed as cold and bleak as the coroner's trestle. An owl's insistent call from the pines behind the cabin was a din within which he could not sleep.

The sheriff sat rifling through a drawer in his desk and Millimaki could hear pens and loose change and perhaps pill bottles and cartridges clattering and then the man said, "Well, shit." He looked up, surprised to see the young man standing there. He sat back and regarded him. "You look about half like a raccoon, Val, with those eyes. You been cattin' around when you get off shift?"

"No, sir. I just haven't figured out how to sleep yet."

"Well, hell. It's not your first graveyard."

Millimaki thought of the bright empty cabin without his wife moving about in her stocking feet, the muffled companionability at the verge of his sleep.

"I slept better when my wife was home. Since she started working, I don't know, it's too quiet."

The sheriff nodded absently. "You'll get it figured out. It takes a while. And about the time you do, it's time to go back to the real world." He looked down at the open drawer once more and then slid it shut. "I've got the finest system in the world for losing shit I need."

Millimaki stood. Out of boredom he'd eaten his lunch too early in his shift and now he felt the bad office coffee eroding the walls of his empty stomach. It churned and creaked and he hoped the sheriff would not hear it.

"Goddamn it, I'm sorry. Your wife's name is . . ."

"Glenda, sir."

"I've got a pretty good system for forgetting shit, too. For Christ sake. Glenda. That's right. She's a nice girl. A nurse, isn't she?"

"Yes, sir. An ICU nurse."

"She been chasing you around when you get home?"

"If she was home she might. Or me her. But she's gone to work by the time I get home."

"Right, right. You just said that."

As if some order in the tumult of papers arrayed across his desktop might be disturbed, he delicately lifted one then another and peered under them. "What is that drive for you, an hour or better?"

"This time of year little over an hour."

"Uh-huh." He patted down his shirt, felt in his pants pockets. He called, "Raylene!" There was no answer from the outer office. "Goddamn it." He picked up a page of paper and held it away from himself and stared at it, scowling.

"You know about Gload, then," he said. "I mean you read his sheet and all that."

"I did some, since we brought him in. I didn't spend a lot of time on it."

"You know there are cops in this town, hell, all over this state, that if they were to pull over John Gload by accident would just about piss their pants? I mean old-time bulls, old-time tough beat cops and sheriffs, sonsofbitches who have seen it all."

Millimaki said, "Officer Dobek did seem a little on edge."

The sheriff smiled grimly. "Not having been there, I can only guess that's a decided understatement."

"But I did hear that about Gload from somewhere, yes, sir." He thought about the old man stiffly astride his chair in the cell and his slow careful trudging along the icy walks, as though afraid in falling he would shatter like crockery. "It's hard to believe now."

"Don't be fooled by that smile, Val, or him being an old man. You've seen those hands. He could squeeze juice out of a stove log."

"Yes, sir. That's true."

"Take his sheet home and look over it. Study it. Hell, it might help you get to sleep, though it's more likely to make you lock all the doors and sit up with your gun in your lap. I think we might finally have him on this thing, but there are a lot of unanswered questions floating around with Gload's name hanging off of them."

He shuffled more papers, patted his pockets again front and rear. "Anyway, the shitty thing is this, Val. I'm keeping you on nights. For one thing that old man has a hard-on about Wexler but also he seems to like you. I don't know what it says about you and maybe I don't want to know. He hates cops. Just hates cops like all get-out. But he talks to you. If you could just keep your ears open or maybe even steer him around to talking about some of the shit you'll read on his sheet." As he spoke the sheriff was variously leaning back and hunching forward in an effort to read the print on the files and forms fanned across his desk. He said finally, "Well. It's a long shot. We might be able to clear up some of these things that have been left unfinished since he showed up in this country. And that was a hell of a long time ago."

"All right."

The sheriff eyed Millimaki. "What the hell is it about you, anyway, and that old killer?"

Millimaki thought for a minute. His head felt fat and his stomach rolled dangerously and his eyes burned. "We talk about farming."

The sheriff stared at him. "Farming."

"Other stuff. But farming, yes, sir."

"Well, I'll be damned." He waved Millimaki away and began running his hands beneath the papers on his desktop, feeling his pockets. "Would you please for the love of Christ ask Raylene when you go out if she's seen my glasses anywhere?"

"Do they look anything at all like the ones you have on your head, sir?"

"Oh, for Christ sake." He reached and took them down and glared at them maliciously and then as if addressing them said, "Lest you think me a fool or a liar, Deputy, I'm one of them who wouldn't ever want to run into John Gload with no bars in front of him."

"I wasn't thinking anything."

They were half-glasses and seemed indeed to not fit the sheriff's handsome face and he set them with distaste on his nose. Over these he looked at Millimaki for a long second. "I don't believe for one minute that you're ever not thinking, Deputy." He opened his drawer again and began to set things in order. "Come and see me next week if I forget to send for you. And disregard that it's eight-thirty in the morning and try a glass of beer when you get home. Used to work for me and near as I can tell I never turned out to be a juicer."

When he came out into the outer room a large woman with voluminous red hair set atop her head with two sticks looked up from her desk. She wore an elaborate betasseled shawl held in place over her capacious bust with a pin of pewter or silver in the shape of the state of Montana and she held the telephone receiver pressed against her shoulder with her chin. When she saw Millimaki she said, "What's he caterwauling about in there?"

"It's nothing. He couldn't find something but then he did."

The woman squinted at him, her head cocked oddly, still clenching the phone to her shoulder. "Them goddamn glasses, am I right?" she said. "If he wasn't so vain and would just get a chain for those things." Her manner was proprietary and kind for all she meant to appear the picture of stern subaltern righteousness. She spoke curtly to someone on the phone. When Millimaki looked back from the door he saw she was smiling.

He had spent one normal evening with his wife, though he found himself dozing off during supper and during conversation, and then in their bed later, even as his wife breathed beside him, he could not sleep. Nor the next day. Knowing the dark confinement awaited him he pottered around the empty cabin in his slippers like a shut-in, the early spring sunlight an admonition or taunt. By the time he resumed his shift at the jail, except for those brief snatches in chairs he had barely slept for thirty-six hours. His wife when she left had not bothered to kiss him good-bye.

Gload said, "Good to see you, Deptee. Where you been hiding?"

"I got called out on a lost hiker."

"Have any luck?"

"I found him, if that's what you mean."

"Found him cold."

"Yes."

"Found another one cold and now you're back on shit duty nursemaiding the old man."

It had become their routine. Gload pulled his chair to the bars and arranged his smoking gear beside him on the floor and on his knee balanced the tin bean can, and the young deputy sat his chair under the bank of lights, their faces long waxen caricatures under the purpled sheen.

Gload said, "All manner of excitement while you were out. Brother Wexler hauled in some dangerous criminals, three kids he caught with a twelve-pack of beer. He put 'em in a cell next to that short-eyes asshole and left 'em. Forgot to call their parents for three hours."

"They were minors in possession," Millimaki said.

Gload smoked within his shadows and continued as if he hadn't heard. "Come and sat here and bragged about it to me." Val could hear the old man's breath quicken. "I could hear that fucking pervert Shoals whispering and one of them boys for a long time crying down there."

"He's a letter-of-the-law man. Those boys were in violation of the MIP laws."

"You'd of cut them loose, wouldn't you of?"

"They had violated the law."

Gload hissed suddenly, "Fuck that. You wouldn't of done it. You'd of taken their beer and followed them home and cut them loose, goddamn it."

Millimaki sat. John Gload was breathing heavily.

"Wexler's the worst kind of asshole. I would bet any money you care to name he was a little picked-on turd his whole life and now he's got just a little bit of whack and he's making everybody pay for it. I seen that kind pretty near my whole life. Thousand bucks says he was a turd all his growing up and now he's getting his paybacks." The killer's hand appeared in the light, ghost-white, pointing down toward the now empty cell where a third-offense child molester had recently slept. "Doing shit like that."

Millimaki knew Wexler was capable of such things and he despised him for it and suddenly he hated all of it, the incremental passing of the hours, the eternal darkness he seemed to reside in, the smell, the pettiness and small cruelties that populated his life. The unnamable tension that was present on the rare occasions these days when he saw his wife, who seemed to feel he had chosen this imprisonment as a way of not seeing her and not dealing with the issues of married life.

"I'm right, ain't I?" Gload said.

"I wouldn't know."

"You wouldn't know," Gload repeated. "Don't fucking bullshit me, Deputy. I thought we were friends."

"We're friends, John, inasmuch as you're in there for possibly killing somebody and I'm out here making sure you stay alive to be punished for it."

There was only their breathing, the sound of the lights. Past the high small windows that fronted the sidewalk and street a brief shadow went. Finally Gload said, "I don't want no more company tonight." He stood up and receded suddenly into the gloom of his concrete cage. "You go on and eat your lunch."

Valentine Millimaki sat for a long moment and then stood and turned. But he heard Gload behind him hiss, "I would put him in a hole in the ground, Val. I would put him under and you nor your dog nor anyone would find his ass until his bones were as white as Custer's."

The voice was one he had not heard from Gload before, had not heard in his life, and he stared into the cell as if he might see this other animal that had taken possession of that place, come from some other more calamitous dark. As suddenly it was gone.

"Go on and have your sandwich now," Gload said. "I'll see you tomorrow."

Gload had been in court all day following and seemed worn out by the day's endeavors. When Val came on shift the old man was asleep on his thin cot.

He ate his lunch in the jail's foyer, leafing through the battered magazines, and afterward filled out some paperwork at the request of the jailer. When he walked back through the corridor of cells he could see from a long way off the smoke materializing from the black of Gload's cell.

He took his accustomed chair. Gload spoke a short while of

the day's events in the courtroom, what the prosecutors had said, what his defender had offered by way of rebuttal.

"You know one of them sonsofbitches used a word I never heard before. Maybe you know it. I wrote it down here on my pad." He turned and reached just beyond lightfall to the tiny desk cantilevered by chain from the wall and took up a yellow legal pad. Oddly elegant writing on the lines and baroque fretwork penciled in the margins of imagined creatures and strange faces that may have been caricatures of courtroom players—lawyers or judge or baliff—elongate and leering like those in a funhouse mirror. Gload ran a finger down among his sentences and stopped, tapping the page, and he cast his eyes toward the hall ceiling lights. "Turpitude." He sat staring at the word, twice underlined, his long sloping horse's brow furrowed in concentration, as if the meaning may have been revealed in his recent dreams if he could only conjure it. Finally he said, "No, I haven't never heard that word."

"I never heard of it either," Valentine said.

Gload smiled at him. "Thought you were some kind of college boy."

"That's one I missed."

"He said, 'This man's life of turpitude' and one other time. Seemed pretty proud of it."

"I've got to go on up for a while," Val said. "Want me to look it up?"

"I'd appreciate it."

The old man listened to the clop and rasp of Millimaki's steps diminishing down the darkened hallway. He tried to remember the dream he had had while he slept earlier and could recall only a chaos of amorphous people aswim in that murky realm wearing each other's heads and loosed in the court were the cobbled beasts of sleep—minotaurs and griffins and creatures seen only in the mythology of men's sleep.

He sat smoking in the dark, reading by its sounds the hour of the night and he was smoking still when the deputy came back. The younger man sat down as before on the ladderback chair and said, "Baseness, vileness, depravity." He had written the words on his palm and he turned it to Gload as proof and turned it so the light would fall on the words, large block letters on the farmboy's hand like jailhouse tattoos. Gload smiled above the cat-eye ember of his cigarette, imagining Val's hand with its message easing up the flannel of his young wife's nightdress.

"Well, thank you. I didn't figure it to be anything that might be complimentary."

"Nope. I guess you could have figured that much."

Gload told the young deputy that he sensed something in the demeanor of the state's attorneys. Above their opened files with their heads inclined together like children at a game, they seemed to have an unusual sense of confidence. His own attorney he thought of as little more than stage dressing. He had done work in the past for Gload and some of his contemporaries, but a proclivity toward fortified wine had much diminished him in the ensuing years, and the papers he compulsively shuffled above the table trembled alarmingly, his handwriting a faltering scrawl that for all its illegibility may have been another language entirely. He sat dwarfed beside John Gload with a fond look on his face, a strange small man of indeterminate age around whose balding head ran a lank fringe of hair like inexpertly dyed tree moss. At the end of the day he laid a hand on Gload's shoulder and went out, to be seen no more until morning.

"I don't think my little friend Calvert C. Benjamin, attorney at law, knows shit from Shinola, Val," Gload said. "Them other guys are holding some kind of hole card, I can tell you that, and he's a man wandering in the dark." He gave Millimaki a hard inquiring look.

"I don't hear a thing, John, swear to God. By the time I come on shift there's just me and the jailer and the janitor, and he's deaf as a rock."

"Yeah. Well."

"Anything the state's guys have, your guy'd have too, John."

"True enough. The sonofabitch might just not know what to do with it. But something's up. I can feel it and I smell White."

Gload looked beyond Millimaki to the small arched windows opposite, high up on the wall, and watched as phantom legs scissored across the rectangle of dull yellow streetlamp. The old barred windows let in the wind with a faint moan and it swayed the tube lights overhead on their chains in a barely audible metallic creaking like the turning of a distant windmill. From somewhere down the line of shadowed cages a man coughed deeply and swore.

Gload said, "The good deputy Dobek stopped by earlier to tell me how I'm going to piss my pants when they drop the trap and that my eyes are going to pooch out of my head and shit like that." He snorted. "Hell, they ain't hung nobody in this state for twenty-four years, he ought to know that. But it was sort of sweet of him to stop off and share all that with me just the same."

"I'm sorry about that, John, I really am."

"I believe friend Wexler was there, too, down the way where I couldn't see him."

Gload beyond the latticework of shadows drew on his cigarette and leaned back, and the shadow line clove his face. His eyes were gone. Smoke in twinned plumes hissed from his nostrils. Down the corridor a lodger coughed again and another in his troubled slumber whimpered like a child and John Gload snorted his facsimile laugh. "The wicked flee where none pursueth," he said. "Even in their sleep."

"Bad dreams," Val said.

"Bad dreams. Right." He paused, nodded his head slowly up and down as if agreeing with some muttered point put forth from the obscured region behind him. He inclined into the light, pointed two fingers at Val with the cigarette clenched between them. "You earn those, Val. They don't just show up on their own."

He blew smoke at the floor, leaned and tipped his ash into the bean can. "When I don't sleep it ain't because of bad dreams. It ain't because of ghosts or nothing like that. So what does that tell you?"

"Don't know."

"I don't know either." He studied the polished concrete between his feet. He looked up. "Yes I do. I know what I am, Val."

He was quiet for a long time. He was about to speak when the man cried out from the grip of his troubled sleep and seemed to wake himself and he was cursed by men in adjacent cells and curses and threats went from cage to cage like an echo. Millimaki stood and went down the corridor a short way and stood listening until the noise slowly subsided and there was nothing to be heard but snoring and soft and regular breathing and over all like a swarm of electric bees the maddening hum of the fluorescents.

When Millimaki returned and resumed his seat, Gload said, "Dying is something I ain't afraid of, Val. Don't worry about that shithead Dobek. For one thing, they won't hang me or shoot me the juice or whatever. I'm too old. That'd be bad press for 'em. Hanging is a young man's deal. Nobody gets any satisfaction from jerking an old man's neck."

He paused to shake out a smoke from his pack and kindle it from the previous one and he did so in the dark as a blind man would, by touch and sound, movements done a thousand times in a thousand darks.

"But I will say this—I don't much care for the idea of dying in lock-up. That's just pitiful. You're dead in a field of other loser cons like you were throwed in a landfill."

"That's only if the family doesn't claim the remains."

"First you got to have family."

"But you have someone, John, right? Your wife, is it? The woman out at your place?"

"Nope," he said. "No one."

"Well, I saw her stuff there. We saw a woman's stuff."

"I ain't saying she wasn't there. But like I told you before— gone."

"She'd come back for that, would she not?"

From the shadows Millimaki heard the faint creaking of the chair as Gload shifted his weight. "No," he said, "she will not come back."

Millimaki said, "You never said. Is it your wife?"

In the ensuing pause it may have been a sigh he heard or it may have been a mere exhale of smoke and then from Gload's private darkness could be heard nothing but the faint crackle of paper and tobacco as the old man drew deeply on his cigarette. Millimaki waited, staring into the shadows, but the conversation seemed to be at an end. For these long weeks since he'd been to Gload's house he imagined the woman back, pottering from lonely room to room and tending her frail blooms in their narrow beds, leaning at a window jamb a hundred times a day to witness her man's return when such a returning was as improbable as resurrection.

"My wife won't come here," Val said. "One time when I first come on the department and that was it. Something about this old building gave her the willies."

"Well, I'm on her side about that."

He'd thought introducing his own wife into the conversation might pry loose from the old man's mouth words of wife and marriage but it would not. Finally he said, "Don't you have some other family somewhere, John?"

Blue smoke rolled into the light as the old man spoke, and his voice was newly animated. "Only one there ever was was my dad and when he died it was really the end of anything you might call a normal life for me."

"When did he die?"

"Oh, well. That had to of been sixty-some years ago now."

"You must have been just a kid."

Gload in a muttering undertone toted the years and decades on his thick fingers and then said, "Sixty-four years ago to be exact. And yeah, I was just a kid, Val. But I remember it clear as yesterday." And he began to talk and the details were, even for Millimaki, vivid as any recent memory and the old man talked without pause for a very long time.

SIX

They lived in east Fergus County on the Judith divide and his father ran a few black cows there in the foothills of the Little Snowies and it was there that Gload did the farming that inspired his dreams, a boy all but running the place while the elder Gload, in lieu of more conventional cash crops, kept the operation afloat primarily through poaching and poker.

At their backs as they drove toward the neighbor's hunting shack, late January of John Gload's thirteenth year, was a tide of charcoal Alberta clouds, vanguard of the storm that would orphan him.

The shack sat in a round hollow among the stunted bull pines of that country, situated to be out of the wind and with an eye toward invisibility. While his father and two other men went about butchering a pair of mule deer does and a calf elk jacklighted some days earlier in the Missouri bottoms, young John Gload sat on an upturned crate, sharpening as needed an eclectic collection of knives, his hands even at that age quick and dexterous and the blades as he passed them over the oiled stone appeared liquid as quicksilver. The men sawed and cut, drinking as they did so from a bottle stood among the chunks of meat on a table cobbled up of lengths of stove wood and a sheet of warped plywood. There were two rank-smelling cots in the shack, pushed to the outer walls to make room for the bloody work and in a dark corner a box of rags where a mongrel bitch lay watching the men through hooded eyes. At intervals she would venture out and lap at the thick black pool growing beneath the table until one or other of the men kicked her away. She looked to be part coyote, her lip curled in a perpetual leer to show wretched teeth the color of clay. Her piebald pups in the box mewled piteously at the sudden cold and young Gload stood over them counting, assessing which would thrive, which would perish.

The storm had reached them even in that sheltered place and it sucked and moaned at the door and sent slender serpents of drift into the room. Each man's shadow loomed and shrank beneath the penduluming lantern. Two propane heaters were set to burn but still the butchers' breath blossomed whitely and when they could no longer feel their hands the work was halted. The boy had hoped to take home one of the pups but instead they carried out only packages of meat haphazardly wrapped in butcher paper and bound with electrical tape, the box weeping a thin vermillion trail atop the snow.

The truck was a 1924 four-cylinder Chevrolet and it veered and slewed like a carnival ride along frozen ruts as they climbed through the slanting snow, the blunted trees on either side stuttering and nodding and when they came up into the open parklands the wind hit them full force. Ice crystals blown through the shrunken doorseals shimmered like mica in the green dash-board glow. Four miles out they became high-centered on a wind-scoured drift. The crust was hard as pavement and the truck with its narrow tires had rolled atop it and then simply dropped. The wind howled and the snow swooped down from the yawing treetops into the clearing and broke against the truck like an ocean surge. His father dug around the tires and the wooden spokes with a spade and he would jump in and gun the engine and move ahead a foot or two and then the truck would sink. John Gload could see his father's face red and glis-tening in the headlights as he drove the spade handle down into the drift. It sank to the blade. He stood up into the light and held the shovel up to indicate the depth and shook his head. Gload remembered that his father's hat had fallen off and his hair stood up crazily above his bone-white forehead. After an hour of digging and rocking the truck and more digging, they had progressed no more than ten feet. Neither could they go back, as the snow filled in what tracks they had made until it appeared as if the Chevy had simply been set down like a toy in the center of the drift. The storm raged out of the north and there was little to the world beyond the twinned cones of light the headlights threw and black pines at the limit of their vision stood cowled and sinister as executioners. His father stood the spade in the drift and clambered into the cab.

"Whew, boy. I think we fell into some kind of a glacier or something. We must of drove around it coming in." He sat in the driver's seat panting and sweating. "I don't think there's no bot-tom to the sonofabitch."

He started the engine to warm them, the laboring cylinders barely audible above the wind yowling at the doors, the grainy snow like locusts seething across the metal of the hood. From beneath the seat his father retrieved a pint bottle of J&B and drank from it.

He told his son he was going to make for a ranch house he knew to be just off to the west. "Just down through this little bit of timber," he said. "It's closer than the shack is." He looked at the boy and smiled. "It's not no more than a little hike." He told his son to stay in the truck and for no reason to get out. If he had to pee use the empty beer bottle that had rolled from under the seat. But wait there for him. Run the engine every little while and keep the window down a crack. In the dash glow he examined the level of the bottle, dropped it into the pocket of his coat and stepped out. With his hand on the door handle he seemed to hesitate, looking once back the way they'd come, once up to the white and swirling heavens and then he'd turned and set off into the storm. Young Gload could see him clearly for a while and then as a dark shape wavering against the black pines and then with his face pressed to the clouded window glass young Gload's father became a part of the dark itself.

"He didn't get too far, Val. I guess he was a little turned around because he wasn't headed for nowhere. Nearest house in that direction, I heard some of them sonsofbitches say, was ten miles, prit-near to Grass Range. By the time they found me I was almost done in myself. I wound up losing toes on this one foot."

Millimaki sat staring down into the cell, hypnotized by the disembodied voice. Gload may have thought the deputy was staring at his foot or merely meant to prove the validity of his story, but he shucked off a worn brown brogan and brown sock and thrust into the slant of light a strange foot, very

white, two-toed, looking more like the foot of a large, strange
bird than a man's.

"They brought me to a ranch house and put me in somebody's bedroom. Guy who owned that little cabin, my dad's
partner, he found me there, come in and called me a little sonofabitch for telling them sheriffs where the meat was. But I hadn't
told them nothing. That cold bastard, kid who just lost his old
man." He sat shaking his head there in the dark. "Wasn't long
after that that I seen them carrying him."

Gload leaned forward into the purple lightfall and Val could
see him studying the floor, his bare, strange, dead-white foot.
Finally he said, "Just a little hike, is what he said. And I always
remembered him sort of hesitating there by the truck and him
knowing I was watching and I think he set off like he was sure
just so I wouldn't be scared. I do believe that to be true. Standing there," Gload said, quietly. "Didn't know north from east."

He had last seen his father carried between two sheriff's
deputies across the drifted ranchyard, just a shutter-blink as
they passed what view he had out the window, left to right
between folds of drapery behind which he sat with his black
and swollen feet in a pan of water. It was a misshapen thing
they carried, as brusquely as you might a hay bale or furniture
piece, and it left in the unblemished snow, when they'd passed
from view, a strange drag trail, as though the two men between
them conveyed a fairy-book dragon, its tail and wingtips
unsteady above the alien snow.

From some distant duct-grate or from the imperfect street-level
windows, a breath of air set Gload's bare lightbulb swaying, the
pull chain tinkling softly and he turned his gaze upward. At the

corners of his eyes were long deep crevasses disappearing into his sparse hairline, and from his chronic sleeplessness, as if drawn with a pen, his inflamed eyes were rimmed with red.

From the endeavor of the long narration and the reliving of the winter night that would re-create him in the world, he seemed depleted. His voice when he at last spoke again was faint and hoarse.

He said, "I went from there to a hospital to an orphanage run by these strange ladies dressed up in black, all in the matter of a few weeks. I gotta say, it was a tough old time for a kid."

"I imagine it was," Millimaki said. "My old man went down for a nap and just kept sleeping and that was bad enough."

Gload stared out through the bars. He sat erect in his chair and raked back the thin strands from his forehead and cleared his throat. "When did this happen?"

"Oh, that's been a year now. Year and a half."

"You lost your old man?"

"Sixty-two years old. Died in his chair."

"That's tough."

"He was a decent man. Had this kind of crazy temper but he only hit me once and I had it coming."

"Died in his chair," Gload said. "And you felt like you should of been there."

"Oh, I don't know. Not so much. My cousin was there to check on him every day."

"Felt like you could of done something to prevent it, I imagine."

Val stared in at the old man. "It just happened. His life was hard."

"Sixty-two years of age. Lost your old man at a young age,

same as me." He paused conspicuously to allow the gravity of kindredship to fill the moment.

"Not all that young," Millimaki said.

Gload went on as if he hadn't heard. "And your mother?" he said. "Where is she?"

"Gone a long time now."

"And I bet she run off on you all, didn't she, same as mine? I bet she skipped out."

Millimaki stood up. "Like I said, it was a long time ago."

Gload's hands appeared. He grasped the bars of his cage and leaned his face into the fluorescent light. "We're just a couple of hard-luck orphans, ain't we, Valentine?"

The old man's face was a smiling deathmask in the hard chemical light. Millimaki excused himself and picked up a small brown sack he'd had beside his chair and down the way Gload could hear him talking to one of the men. He came back shortly and set down his bag and settled into the chair. Gload raised an inquisitive eyebrow.

"This Grogan's got some kind of croup. I been giving him some cough dope from home. The store-bought stuff doesn't seem to be doing much."

"Like a goddamn TB ward in here," Gload said. "Been listening to him cough up his lungs all day." He sat slowly pulling on his sock, lacing his shoe, and with a cigarette stuck in the corner of his mouth he studied the young deputy. "Goddamn bleeding-heart cop. Christ on a crutch." He snorted, shook his head in amused disbelief. Smoke plumed from his nostrils. He wiped the toe of each shoe on the back of his dungarees and examined them in the light.

He said, "What time you got, Val?"

"It's a little after one. Ten after." Millimaki consulted his watch and as he did the clock in the Catholic church three blocks away tolled once. "There you go. I might be a little fast."

"Did you eat yet?"

"I did. Just before I came in."

Gload considered this. He stood and moved his chair next to the bars and arranged his smoking gear on the floor and rested the bean can on his knee.

"Why don't you move over just a bit closer, Val, so we don't keep these assholes awake. Unless you got things to do."

Val checked his watch again out of habit and sat with his head cocked, listening for a moment to the sleeping corridor. Grogan slept on, the others slept or silently listened. "Not really," he said. He picked up his chair and carried it nearer the bars, just beyond arm's reach. He settled it there, sat and crossed his legs, and in the shadows Gload, still watching, smiled.

"Still don't trust the old man, Val."

"Policy, John. You ought to know that."

Gload leaned forward just enough to meet the deputy's eyes. His look was fond. "Val, I'm going to tell you some things and you can tell the Old Bull but I suspect it won't make no difference to me at this point."

"You know I'd be obligated to report anything concerning illegal activities, so you maybe want to just stick to safe subjects."

"Policy."

"However you want to call it."

"Well, you let me worry about it, Val."

"I just want to be clear on that."

"You are perfectly clear, Deputy."

"Okay."

Having shifted forward, Gload now sat half in light, half in dark, and he looked to have been sheared in two and set for display, head and shoulders of a taxidermied felon, a trophy displayed for tourists or schoolchildren in a diorama of prison life: table, chair, cot. Killer.

He lasted no more than six months at the Catholic orphanage where he was remanded as a ward of the neighboring state where the bones of his mother were buried. The first months there were marked by long gloomy silences and merciless teasing as the boy sought for his solitude the comforting dark of closets and gardening sheds and kitchen pantries. Then he began to fight. For young John Gload there was nothing of sport in these contests, and almost from the first, blood was the common consequence, as if like some pagan sacrament they could not be otherwise consummated. Boys three and four years older and twenty pounds heavier went about with torn ears and gouged eyes, the corners of their mouths split where Gload had jammed in his fingers and simply pulled, as though trying to tear a gunnysack. The screams of his dorm mates or threats from nuns or priests went unheard and Gload was more than once blindsided with a sap by one of the tough old Jesuits as he worked blood-speckled and stoical atop a boy who may have simply laughed at the wrong time.

Few of the residents or staff was saddened by his departure and when he set out under a shard of moon wending westward on his barely healed feet he was neither sought nor reported missing. He progressed across that state afoot and by car. He shared the back of a pickup with a six-year-old girl alone with her 4-H hog which was so huge it might have crushed and eaten her. He rode in an Oldsmobile with a candy salesman from

Duluth, Minnesota, who offered him twenty dollars to show his underwear. There were two phlegmatic wheat farmers, brothers and perhaps twins, so preoccupied with the clouds marshaled in the skies over Canada just to the north that they abandoned the road altogether and drove cross-country through fallow and farm toward a strange metal structure bristling with antennae which they called the Weather Temple of Christ Jesus and offered to let him stay and pray if he could prove the purity of his heart and he rode with a half-mad rancher's wife abroad at midday drinking, who would have killed them both on a bridge abutment had not Gload taken the wheel as she nodded into unconsciousness. By these and other such means he crossed the border back into the state of Montana in the summer of 1947.

In the little town he arrived at that afternoon, boys his age on bicycles stared after him and there were boys walking toward the river with fishing poles on their shoulders and except for the filthiness of his clothes and the look of the wolf in his eye he may have been just another of them.

He was hot and tired, having walked several miles that morning from the highway where a car had dropped him off. The air was syrupy with the smell of roadside sweet clover and his pants cuffs were yellow from it as though he'd walked through a field of chalk.

He had seen her as he passed down a neighborhood, an older woman in her bathrobe kneeling on a gardening pad behind a wire fence and turning the soil in her flowerbeds with a hand trowel. A tiny ivory Pomeranian attended her and sat panting in the shade of a lilac. Gload went down the street and returned and as he did he saw her get up and put her hands to the small of her back and look up at the sun. She bent to speak to the dog and it rose and began yammering and running in circles like a wind-up toy.

He went in through a back gate, pausing under a hanging feeder where small yellow birds fluttered, raining tiny seeds down on him. A bird flew up onto an overhead branch gaudy with purple plum blossom and began a long sweet canzonet as if in greeting.

He went silently in the door and among the rooms looking for he knew not what. He pocketed a hairbrush, a watch, change from a china bowl on a nightstand. He felt comfortable there, as though these smells and plaster saints and faintly ticking and chiming clocks were the things of his own childhood, the ghosts of forgotten longings. When the old woman came into the room, young John Gload stood before a mantelpiece studying the faces in framed photographs as though among those grainy images he might find his own staring back. She did not speak but only gazed openmouthed to find this ragged boy in her house. The Pomeranian began to yelp and it lunged and sank its needle teeth into John Gload's bare ankle and without thinking he snatched it up and threw it against the wall. It was only then she began to scream. Young Gload in one motion picked up a table lamp, swung, and hit her above her left ear with its heavy leaded base. He was surprised that she went down as hard and as fast as she did and she lay on the carpet in the summer sunlight perfectly still.

He set down the lamp on the table, aligning it in the dustless circle where it had stood and he looked at his hands. He studied the small crimson mark on the wall where the dog had struck, a small runic daub like a cave marking, and he stood above the clutch of animated rag where it lay working its obscene little mouth soundlessly.

Finally he stood over the woman. She was very pale and lay with her arms outthrown and one leg crossed beneath her as though she had only misstepped while dancing. Kneeling, he opened her robe and carefully straightened her long limbs, so light, he thought, as if the bones of her had already begun to go to dust. He raised her pale shift and examined the parts of her that boys at the orphanage had whispered about and he'd seen in nudist magazines some of them kept hidden from the nuns. He lay atop her fully clothed and after a while he put his arms around her and he spoke to her, said the name of one of the girls from the sister orphanage he'd once danced with and he said some of the things the other boys said in the locker room after gym class. The woman's eyes were half-closed and from one nostril a single drop like a viscous red tear appeared.

He stood up. The little Pom dog lay as before and made a snoring sound and then was still, one eye agape, slightly bulged and aglow from the long afternoon sunrays breaching the gauzy curtains. He looked at the woman again and presently went to her and arranged the folds of her robe over her breasts and withered limbs. There was a small pillow on the sofa, a purfling of white lace for a border and incomprehensible words lovingly needlepointed across its face. He placed it under her head and but for the blood at her nose and the crease above her ear that had by then begun to leak a crimson pool beside her, she may well have been asleep.

In the kitchen he stopped and chose an apple from a turned wooden bowl and he stood in that bright clean room looking at the apple in his hand. He set it on the counter, returned to the outer room. Rummaging in a drawer he found a pair of men's socks and he dabbed at the blood on his ankle with them and put them on. Passing the woman again he paused, looking down.

He took the pillow from under her head and placed it over her face, reading again the words stitched there—foreign, hopelessly untranslatable, and for all that unforgettable, as he felt they were meant to convey a message, tidings as obscure and cataclysmic as the goldfinch's song.

Leaving, he took the apple from the counter, closed and locked the door, and walked west progressing unhurriedly in his strangely nautical gait under an arcature of ponderous elms, more birdsong in his ears.

When he had finished his long narrative, the old man sat back stiffly with a barely audible groan, whether the protest of chair slats or of old bones Millimaki could not tell. He straightened in his own seat and was himself stiff and when he checked his watch from long habit he realized his shift was nearly up. His stomach creaked and turned. The corridor was brighter now with the marginal light from the high windows, and the new day was announced with the sound of men urinating and the striking of matches. Grogan had begun to cough.

Gload seemed to have gone far away in conjuring such memories and from his private darkness he was a long time speaking. Finally he leaned his long face out into the purple light and raised his eyes to look at the deputy as if he might read something in the younger man's face.

"Funny, ain't it, Val, I started out the way I did on account of a little Pom dog?"

"Wait," Val said. "An apple? You ate an apple?"

"An apple, why not? Yeah. That's not important, Val, but here's the deal." He sat with his forearms upon his knees, gazing into the palms of his enormous hands as if recorded there among the ridges and cracks was the transcript of his life and he was merely reading it aloud. "Along about two miles later I sat down on a railroad berm to catch my breath. It was an interesting moment. By the time I ate that apple, I didn't feel a thing about that woman." He rolled his eyes up to regard Millimaki, his hands still open on his knees in a sort of offertory pose. "Val, I knew right then I'd never in my life have to do a regular day of work again."

trelliswork of brush to the small creek. She took his hand mutely. At the bank they stretched out in the grass, the burbling lullaby of the water in their ears. In a very short time he fell asleep. He awoke from a sumptuous dreamless nap and Glenda was gone. He found her in the car, curled on the backseat like a child. He got in and eased shut the door. She did not wake, or pretended not to, as he drove home through a cool blue light descended upon the canyon. Above, the day diminished in a brilliant unfurling of color, the tottering pines atop the ridges as vivid as candle flames.

The little car rattled and bumped slowly once again up the hill to the unlit cabin. Millimaki stood leaning on the hood of the car for its warmth and his wife lay as before on the rear seat. The dog had come to the wire of his kennel and he whimpered softly.

As Val stood, dusk went to dark. From among the crevasses in the coulee rimrock to the south bats emerged by the hundreds and they swarmed among the constellations burning coldly through the black palisade of the pines. The single yard light had flickered on. He went to the rear door to wake her. She lay with one hand beneath her head and he stood looking at her through the dusty window glass. In the queer light she looked made of wax.

EIGHT

As he'd been instructed, Val after his shift the following week reported to the sheriff's office where he was ushered into the inner sanctum by the secretary with a brief backhand wave, the woman's eyes, inches from her monitor's screen, blank and iridescent as an insect's. Within, Millimaki stood before the man's desk with its bedlam of paper and plastic bags with esoteric articles enclosed and he felt a sudden pang of guilt, as though he were about to violate some priestly pact.

The sheriff regarded him over the top of his half-glasses. He said, "Did I send for you?"

"Sort of, sir. You told me last week to come and talk to you. About Gload. You said if I heard anything."

The man stared at Val critically. "It would seem the remedy I recommended for your malady has failed to work."

"I've been trying it. For some reason drinking beer that early in the day gives me a headache."

"It's not early, exactly, when you're on graveyards. For Christ sake, it's Miller Time."

"I can't get my head to figure that out."

The sheriff wagged his head sadly and the glasses that seemed so out of place on his face slid to the end of his nose. He pushed them up and leaned his head back to study the younger man through the magnifying lenses, as if that scumbled focus might present a more lucid picture.

"You still partnered up with that old man?" he said.

"I guess so."

"You must be his long-lost spawn, for Christ sake. I never knew of him to say much more than two words to any uniform and those two were 'Fuck you.'"

"I can't explain it."

"On top of that he's been talking to Wexler and that really puzzles me. Maybe the old sonofabitch is getting soft. Or soft in the head."

"I didn't know that."

"That he was talking to Wexler or soft in the head?"

"Wexler."

"He never mentioned it?"

"Well, just that Wexler had been to see him. Not so much that he was really talking to him."

"Maybe he doesn't want to hurt your feelings."

Val didn't say anything. The sheriff busied himself with the mess atop his desk.

"So what do you have?"

"He told me about an old woman he killed."

"The hell he did." The older man took down the glasses and set them among the papers strewn on his desk. He was suddenly interested. He rifled through the top desk drawer and came up with a small brown pipe, looked into its bowl and put the stem in the corner of his mouth.

"Yes he did."

"Terrific. Did you see anything on his sheet about it?"

Millimaki held his wrists crossed before him and he held his cap by the brim and stood staring at the county logo on the face of it. "I don't know if this is what you had in mind when you said to come in, sir."

"Well, you let me decide that, Deputy."

"It was over east, in Wibaux, I think."

"And? That doesn't make any difference."

Val looked out the window. "He was fourteen."

"Fourteen years old."

"Yes, sir."

"Christ, that had to have been, what, sixty-some years ago?"

"Sixty-five."

"Well, that doesn't do us a lot of good, does it?"

Millimaki stood fingering the bill of his cap. "He said it didn't bother him. Not for long, anyway."

"Well, that's our boy."

"That he saw after that he wouldn't have to do real work ever again."

The sheriff sat back in his chair. "The beginning of a long and colorful career." He placed his hands together beneath his chin as if in prayer, steepled his index fingers as in the child's game. He ran his eyes over the thin sallow figure of the young deputy.

"And how is Gail?" he said.

"She's okay. It's actually Glenda."

"For Christ sake, of course it is."

"Fine. She's fine."

The sheriff stared at him. Val looked toward the single window, high and arched and brilliant in the early morning despite the calligraphy of water streaks and splashes of bird shit from the vile and mumbling pigeons roosted in the rain gutters at the roof edge. Because it had once been part of the jail itself, there were bars on the window, and their shadows lay across the floor and laddered the far wall.

"Your mouth says fine but your face says otherwise."

"She's having a hard time with me being on nights."

"Harder than you."

"Harder than me, yessir. I think so."

"It's tough. I know. I did it. We all did it."

"I know. I'm not asking for anything."

"I know you're not. I couldn't hardly change things, anyway, Val. It's all low-man-on-the-totem-pole stuff. You know that, don't you?"

"I do."

"This might not be the best analogy, but it's kind of like breaking a horse. It's tough on everybody at first and then pretty quick all parties involved don't think anything of it. It's just how it is."

"I might choose to not tell her that comparison if it's all the same to you."

"My wife if she heard it would leave me singing like Liberace for a week. For some reason women don't like being compared to livestock." He removed the cold pipe from his mouth and sat looking at it. "And that might be the extent of my wisdom on the matter."

"That's more than some."

The sheriff smiled. "More than some, yes it is." He put the pipe in his mouth again and began to pass his hands over the mess of files and paper on his desk as if waiting for one or the other to insinuate its urgency. He said, "Do you feel the need to take some time off? I could arrange that."

"No, sir. It'll be all right. Plus, I don't think it's a good time to lay off as far as Gload's concerned."

"Well, as far as that goes, I don't think it matters. It looks pretty good we've got him on this guy up north of town."

"I didn't know that."

"You read his M.O. on making his guys anonymous, did you not?"

"Where he takes the teeth and hands? Did he not do it this time?"

"Oh, no. Our boy is thorough. It isn't that. But it seems this poor kid had had open-heart surgery here a while back. Two years and some. What they're saying is that they can identify him by the way he was put back together. The chest-crackers have a kind of signature way of wiring them back up."

"I didn't know that."

"Hell, I didn't either. And safe to say John Gload didn't or he'd have carved the chest right out of him and thrown that in the drink, too."

"Is that what he did with the head and stuff?"

"What the kid White said. Threw them over the dam. Hell, that head's probably rolling along outside of St. Louis by now." The sheriff pointed his pipestem vaguely out the window to indicate where that city lay. "Anyway, your old boy's going away until he dies. It would be nice to know where all the bodies are buried—metaphorical and otherwise—but you don't have to milk him anymore if you don't want. He's had it." He looked down, selected an envelope seemingly at random and studied it through the half-lenses of his small glasses. He said, "The *end* of a long and colorful career."

"I guess so."

The sheriff laid the envelope down and became preoccupied with some other and he turned his head oddly to read it as though it were fixed to the desktop and could not be turned. He rested his elbows atop the clutter and held the pipe by its bowl in one hand and sat reading. Millimaki stood quietly. Then he put his cap on.

The sheriff did not look up. "Remember what he is, Val. Think of what he did to that young man out there and how he did it and how many others he did the same way. He doesn't deserve your pity."

"Yes, sir."

He was almost out the door when the sheriff said, "And, Val. That was good work on the old boy with the Buick or Pontiac or whatever it was. His family was very grateful."

"Buick, sir. And it wasn't anything, really. He didn't get too far and Tom went right to him."

"Well." The sheriff laid his pipe carefully on the jumble atop his desk, as if it might shatter or disturb some order there known only to him. "How long has it been?"

"Fifteen months and a couple weeks. Or thereabouts. Not that I'm counting."

"You'll get past this streak, Val. It all equals out."

"How so?"

"Hell, I don't know. Just that some you find alive who should be dead. Some you find dead after a warm night in the trees with nothing more than a bruise on their shin."

"With all due respect, sir, that doesn't even make sense."

"It doesn't have to make sense, son. You should know that much by now. But it's the way it is."

"I'll just have to trust you on that point, sir."

"You do that." He took up the unlit pipe and stuck it in his mouth and waved Millimaki away. "Now go home and be nice to your wife."

That day he forsook his routine beside the river and drove north of town to view the scene of the disinterment. The yellow crime scene tape had been left or forgotten and it writhed among the weed bines like some exotic jungle viper and flapped and snapped in the wind. He sat on the ground near the very place John Gload had stood conducting the young man's burial with the barrel of his pistol. Millimaki could see where the hole had been, the earth dished and dark from having been so recently turned and much of it had been sifted for evidence. It lay at the edges of the hole as fine as talc. He imagined the thing they'd dug up would have been, after two months, no more than a rawhide headless mannequin, the incriminating Frankenstein scar at its breastbone hidden beneath dirty rags. For John Gload there would have been much sawing and twisting, stubborn elastic tendons to be cut or bent over a knee and snapped. Vertebrae would have to be unlocked, the head twisted. He tried to imagine the sound. Little blood had been found at the scene, so Gload must have bled the victim somewhere else. There had been a time, he thought, not long ago, when coyotes had come tacking out of the night with the alien scent in their nostrils to roll in the gore and muddy their teeth.

He took up a handful of dirt and let it sift through his fingers. The wind came down from the northern benchlands and rattled the strange larval pods on the yuccas and brought the faint thin cries of gulls he could see afloat and stationary as kites against the morning sky. He tried to reconcile the avuncular old man tendering comfort and counsel from his dark cage with the creature who could placidly dismember a fellow human being. A lifetime ago while eating an apple (an apple, Val thought, like me that day, eating that apple) beside railroad tracks on a golden spring day, John Gload had observed in himself with a curious detachment the absence of passion. Perhaps he was somehow exempt from responsibility at all, could no more be blamed than a child born without feet could be blamed for his inability to run.

Millimaki sat in the dirt staring blankly at the grave, benumbed by his sleeplessness. Gload seemed capable of kindness, but it may have been just a kind of vestigial feature, like the webbed and blunted limbs of thalidomide children—a half-developed grotesquery that made him more pitiable for the reminder of what it might have been like to be whole.

For the rest of us though, thought Millimaki, the distance from reason to rage is short, a frontier as thin as parchment and as frail, restraining the monster. It was there in everyone, he thought. It was there in himself. A half second of simple blind fury and the hatchet falls down. He stared at the patch of turned earth where so recently a body had been. At some point, he thought wearily, it was only meat.

He sat for some time, the wind coursing through the sparse bluestem and whipping the yellow tape. His pallid hands were in his lap and he stared into them. The sun felt good on his face and he closed his eyes. Fifteen minutes later he woke with a start. He'd fallen asleep sprawled in the grass above the grave and when he raised up there was dirt stuck to the side of his face and one arm was numb and dead. He sat up looking around wildly, as if someone might have crept up on him in that lonesome place. "For Christ sake," he said aloud. "Look at your ass, sleeping in the dirt like a bindlestiff."

The weeds had grown up in the road between the wheel ruts and they hissed along the undercarriage as he climbed toward the cabin. On the opposite coulee side among the rimrocks, marmots scuttled and froze and it appeared at that distance that the rocks themselves moved. The church-steeple tops of the lodgepole behind the little house quaked in the wind. His wife's car was still in its place and he could see Tom pacing in his kennel. He parked and walked across to the dog run. The shepherd sat and whined. "Hey kid, how you doing?" He stroked the dog's nose with two fingers through the chain link. He looked toward the house, and the windows in the early sunlight dazzled his tired eyes.

He went in and hung his hat on a 16-penny nail driven into a wall log and when he turned he saw her standing at the sink in her street clothes and she didn't look at him.

"Hey," he said, "how come you're not at work?"

"It's my day off. You should know that."

"Is it Tuesday? Man, my head-clock is all screwed up."

"Your everything is screwed up, Val."

He expected her to turn and laugh but she did not.

"What's Tom doing locked up?"

She didn't answer.

"Glenda," he said, "why's the dog penned?"

She spoke to the window. "Because he kept following me around." There were no dishes in the sink and no water running. She stood gripping the counter edge. "Every time I made a trip to the car he followed me and he followed me back and I just got tired of it."

He stood for a while looking at her and then walked onto the porch. He could see boxes jumbled in the backseat of the Datsun and clothes hanging from the hooks above each side window. He went back in and stood behind her. The window was a bright rectangle framed with box elder trees and the coulee rim beyond was green with spring and the sky the kind of blue, with its Van Gogh brushstrokes of cloud, that had made them, in the early years, jump in the truck and drive the country with no purpose whatever. It was enough to be together under the spring sun in the greening and open country. He stood looking out at it, over her shoulder. Her yellow hair glowed with the sun in it and he suddenly wanted to take it in his hands, press it to his face.

"It's a driving and-drinking sky we got today."

She studied her hands before her, glanced up briefly to the perfect day. She said, "Where have you been? You should have been home two hours ago."

He made a wiping motion across his face. There was still a trace of dirt on his cheek and in his hair. "I had to go up north of town and look at a site. Really, I forgot it was your day off."

"A site," she said.

"We found a body up there."

She turned then and he could see she had been crying. "Oh. Well. A body. That's okay. At least someone you can relate to."

"What's going on, Glenda?"

She looked at him. "What's on your face? Jesus, Val, you look like a homeless man."

He said, "I want you to tell me what's going on."

"I'm going to stay in town."

"Tonight?"

"Tonight. For a while."

"How long a while?" Millimaki said.

"I don't know. Indefinitely." She put the back of one wrist to each eye in turn and swept back her hair as though to put herself right. "I would have to say indefinitely."

"You seem to have it all mapped out," he said. "Isn't this something that we ought to have at least talked about beforehand? For Christ sake, Glenda."

"I tried to talk about it but every time I looked up you were asleep or on some other planet."

"That might be a little bit true, but goddamn it, I can't sleep anymore."

"But it's more than that."

"More than what?"

"More than your emotional absence."

He looked at her. She had composed herself in earnest and stonily studied a point above his head. "That sounds like something out of a book," he said.

"It describes our situation."

"When did this turn into a situation? For Christ sake, I come home and take off my hat and I'm in a situation."

"All I know is I can't think here and I have to have time to think."

"You've got all the time in the world for that."

"You're not listening, goddamn it. I said I can't think *here*."

"Why not? I thought you loved it here. You've said that any number of times. This is your house, goddamn it."

"I can't think." She enunciated each word slowly, as if she spoke to a foreigner or a lip reader. "And I feel small."

"All this goddamn thinking," Val said. He rubbed his hand over his face. He felt dull, his arms heavy as stones. He stared at her. Everything she said—her posture, the set of her jaw as she

spoke to somewhere beyond him—seemed rehearsed. Millimaki in his fatigue fought the feeling that two other people
were playing this scene, their doppelgängers, while he and his
wife stood to the side merely watching.

"What's all this goddamn thinking about?"

"Well, there it is. You don't even know."

"Okay," he said. He ran his hand in a washing motion over
his face again. "Okay, what do you mean 'small'? Let's start with
that. That doesn't even make any sense to me."

"It means I feel unimportant. In your life and just in general.
And it's exacerbated by this place. I feel like it's swallowing
me up."

He reached out to touch her crossed arms, to make some
contact while reason and his own center were flying about the
room. She took a half step away.

"That's not one of your words," he said. "It doesn't even sound
right coming out of your mouth."

"It means it makes it worse here."

"I know what the fuck it means. But you're not the one saying it."

Her words came in an exaggerated calm, as though to coun-
teract his urgency. The room darkened suddenly, whether from
a passing cloud or from some dimming behind his tortured eyes
he could not tell. The exertion of mustering reason sufficient
to the moment was enormous and his head swam.

"I need to have time to think and I can't do that here, now.
That's what I'm saying."

"You said it's swallowing you up."

"It is. Without you here I'm more alone than alone." This
thought seemed to suddenly attenuate her resolve and she began
to cry again. "You don't know. You couldn't, because it's so much

a part of who you are. But not me, not by myself." She repeated, "You don't know."

"What? What don't I know?"

"At night. At night. It's awful."

"Why?"

She'd evidently not planned to let the conversation go this way and she paused to consider her words. "At night, outside the house is inside with me. It comes in with me and it's like I can look down at myself and all I see is me in the bed and there's nothing between me and everything out there." She swept her hand toward the bright day. "Val, you don't know. You couldn't know. I've been sleeping with all the lights on. And don't you dare say anything. One night an owl was in the house."

"That's just crazy."

"I told you, don't say it."

"There isn't a way for it to come in here, Glenda."

"It was above the bed and it was just up there and beating the air with its wings. Fanning the air."

"For Christ sake."

She covered her face. "I could feel the air moving."

"No. It couldn't have come in the house."

"And then last night, on the porch, there were coyotes."

"It's just nightmares, Glenda."

"Don't."

"For Christ sake, Tom would have gone ape-shit if coyotes were on the porch."

She pointed toward the front door as if to present concrete proof and he could see her hand trembling. "I heard their toe-nails on that porch, Val. I heard them breathing."

"No. They wouldn't come up there."

"Clicking. A clicking sound." Her hand went to her mouth. "And that fucking door. They could have just pushed on it and come in."

"Okay, listen. It's nothing. It's the branches on that box elder rubbing against the house. That's all it was, Glenda. I'll cut them back. Right now, today. Just branches in the wind. I'll cut them all the way back."

"Not branches," she said. "Or the wind or anything. You will not talk me out of this because I know what I know."

Millimaki closed his eyes. He felt behind him for the arm of the couch and sat down heavily on it. He said, "Glenda, I'm absolutely all in. I can't find my own ass with both hands. Can't we just talk about this tomorrow? I just need to sleep. This isn't fair right now. I can't figure out what it's all about."

"It's about what I said it's about. That's easy enough, isn't it? I can't stay here. When we had it together, I felt above it or at least a part of it. But alone here I'm no more important than a bird or a tree. Whether it's a nightmare or whether it's real, what it means is that this place is swallowing me up. It's a part of you, Val, but it's swallowing me up. The more you fade the more it swallows me up."

Val looked at her bleakly. "You act like I'm a ghost. I'm your husband. I'm sitting right here."

"No. You're right, that's perfect. That's exactly what you are. A ghost." She took a long deep breath, seeking oxygen where it seemed in insufficient supply, and released it slowly. "And I don't know where you are, Val. I think probably out with all the dead people you find out there. They're easier. You don't have to talk to them. You bring home their goddamn pictures like they were family or some secret girlfriend. Jesus Christ, Val, that's what you are, no more than a ghost yourself, walking around with all those dead people in your head. I won't stay with a ghost, Val. I won't do that. And I won't become one myself."

When she had gone, Val stood with his coffee out on the porch in the dizzying light of late morning. He had moved about the kitchen woodenly as if in a dream and his hands seemed to him pale creatures crabbing among the cups and plates of their own accord. He realized as he stood at the sink that she must have watched him drive up and move around the yard and to the kennel and mount the stairs with his slow geriatric tread. He tried to make out in the window glass the face of the stranger she'd said inhabited her husband's skin and saw in the silvery pane a parody of himself, got up in fard and eye black and wrinkled khaki, who in wearily ascending the steps entered the middle act of a pedestrian tragedy. Or worse, he thought, she'd seen the ghost of the man she had married, no more than a bleared outline of opaque glass in her husband's shape through which she could see the grass, the dirt, the trees beyond.

Far below through the greening trees he could almost see the place along the creek where they'd swum one afternoon in their courting days. To get there they pushed through undergrowth and came out near the creek and from the tall grass and thin willow stems at their elbows rose a cloud of small orange butterflies and they went before them on the warm air like a blizzard of flower petals strewn before heroes. The stream swung fast and clear out of impenetrable brush as if emerging from a cave, curved languidly and pushed murmuring against a steep cutbank where the roots of a toppled cottonwood splayed above the current. They spread a blanket on the warm sandy shingle and while Val was making a fire he heard a splash and saw her golden head bobbing with the current and then as he watched she rose glistening from the stream below the bend like some fabled huntress, dripping and naked and all but aglow from the sun and the cold water. He stood with a stick in his hand staring foolishly. From habit, as he'd done as a boy when there was something he desperately wanted, he said a prayer: dear God let this woman stay with me, let me not ruin this, let her marry me and I will be good and pure forever and then as she came on, placing her tender feet carefully on the gravel, milk-white skin bejeweled in the sun, all prayers evaporated and in the center of all the universe was only her. And he would at that moment have done anything to have her.

Now as he stood on the porch he realized he would do it yet, if he could only discover the correct god, tender the proper coin. He gazed at the creek far below, chromium glintings through the cottonwood and willow. He slung the coffee out onto the dirt. The dog Tom from the fenced run sat watching him and when Millimaki went inside he turned to stare down the narrow lane where the car had passed and where a veil of dust hovered yet above the tracks like mist. In the creek bottom the crowns of the cottonwood trees were gilded by the sun's rising above the coulee rim, so bright and substantial they looked to have been held by the roots and dipped in a vat of molten gold. Sparrows had come to peck like yardfowl in the spare expanse of lawn and their shadows lay long across the grass in the shape of exotic giants—egrets, flamingos.

In the coming days and nights he went about his duties mechanically and at home he could not bring himself to sleep in the empty bed. He awoke late afternoons dull and sore from the recliner or the couch and found the only thing good about his life then was that he did not have to speak to a living soul. Even

Gload left him to his thoughts during his interminable shift and required from him only his presence, as if like a hearth fire the young man's bleak thoughts and brooding were a comfort to him. He sat for many hours beyond the bars transfixed by the disembodied brutal hands hanging in the light and before long they began to articulate some feeling within him. Sitting around the cabin in the mercurial spring days among his wife's things, the scent of her still lingering in the bedding and closets, he found to his horror that he missed the old man's company.

He watched the storms roll in from the west, erasing the sun as fully as an eclipse, and then the rain slashed down, ripping at the new leaves on the box elder and lilacs and gouging troughs in the road. Then as suddenly the day was brilliant again, even as the rain sluiced from the porch roof in an effulgent cataract. Looking out it was as though the two hemispheres of his brain were at war, each eye viewing different worlds—one brilliant, the other black and violent. What peace he had came upon him in the mausolean dark in the company of caged men where speech was not required of him—there among sociopaths he was disburdened of the weight of sociability.

Once during this time he called his wife. While he waited for her to take the phone he could hear through the vacant earpiece garbled voices speaking the idiolect of the ICU. Another language entirely to speak of the ill and dying. When she came on the line he realized that he had nothing to say. He asked how she was. She was fine. He asked when she could be coming home. She didn't know. Silence. He pictured her standing impatiently at the nurses' station, beyond her the enshadowed ranks of beds and their still tenants in thin cotton habiliment festooned with luminous tubes. For reasons he wasn't sure of, he told her he and the dog had found a young girl in the river who had been raped and strangled. It wasn't true. After a pause she said, "How awful." Someone spoke to her and he heard her say, "Bed Seven," and she said to him, "Val, I've got to go now."

"She was eight, this girl. Did I say that?"

"Yes. I'm sorry. I have to go, Val."

"All right."

"I'll see you."

"You'll see me when?"

"I can't say a time. I'll just see you."

"I could come by there."

"No," she said. "That's not a good idea, Val."

"Then come by the jail. I've got nothing but time there."

"Val, you know I hate that place. I won't come there."

"I know."

"Val. I have to go."

"Fine."

He waited for her to say something more. In the long pause before she ended the connection he could hear in the background the chirps and bleeps of the machines that became for the people lying there as much a part of them as their skin or veins. He waited. He heard a man's voice say her name and then she was gone.

From the couch among his twisted bedclothes he heard the tree limbs rubbing along the house eaves, a sound that to her had been the vile nails of predators seeking her innermost part was for him a balm and a caress on his troubled ear. Nothing, though, seemed to touch his sleeplessness. It was as durable as stone and had become as chronic as Gload's but without even the soporific of the plowed fields of his youth to remedy it. He considered her accusation that he consorted with ghosts and it was certainly true. But the dead were a part of her work, too.

She seemed to be able to leave them, though, and at the moment
of their passing they became as inanimate finally as the burbling
machines whose tubes and wires were meant to keep them
alive. She'd told him that they were gone for her then and that
was the end of it. And in telling him he sensed even an animos-
ity toward them as if, as the unreliable cog in the mechanism,
they had betrayed her. She was not to be blamed for wanting to
forget her failures. Certainly, he thought, some of it was professional bluster, but still she seemed as dispassionate in her way as
Gload. He envied them both.

But he was at home with the dead, she was right. And whether
they sought the open country for their death, or death sought
them there, it little mattered. In either case kindred souls, Millimaki and the dead, met under a companionable sky and the
encounter was good for all. In the reticence of their company
Millimaki found peace and for their part the dead would be
brought home to rest among their kin beneath the verdancy
and perdurable headstones of cemeteries. Their bones would
not be gnawed and broadcast like fallen branches down anonymous canyons. And that, too, was a comfort to him.

Without the woman around and in the absence of work in
the woods, the dog Tom became possessive and if Val stood
anywhere for any length of time came to nuzzle his hand. He
took the dog walking in the trees behind the house and Tom
loped ahead, leaping and running his nose under the leaves and
pine duff and then came back and went to heel when he saw Val
unaccountably standing still as stone, as if he required guid-
ance through foreign terrain.

NINE

Seen from the street they may have been a young man and his grandfather, taking the spring air among the elms in pale leaf. Millimaki in escorting the old man back to his cell at day's end allowed him to sit on one of the benches in the courthouse park and smoke. They sat side by side, Gload in his orange county jumpsuit emblazoned with PRISONER on its back and the deputy with his arms over the bench back listening. The great gray trees and the wind in them moving the leaves seemed to evoke memories in the old man and he sat with his cuffed wrists upon his knees and he would occasionally lift his head and draw in a great breath and expel it, savoring the air of freedom as though from a mine shaft he had risen to safety from the corrosive dark.

Val took the old man's Camels from the breast pocket of the garish suit and shook one out and when Gload selected one he lit it for him. They sat watching the cars pass on the street and the birds flare overhead. Finally Millimaki said, "John, you know Sid White took them to a body up north of town."

Gload sat with his head back following the birds with his eyes. He raised his paired hands to his lips and drew on the cigarette, expelling a long slow plume.

"Yeah, I heard that."

"They're saying they can tie you to this guy."

The old man lowered his head and sat erect and strangely formal, staring into the middle distance. "Don't think so, Val," he said. "They can't bank their whole case on White. For one, he's got a record. Not what you might call a credible witness." He snorted, shook his head in disgust, or amusement. "And look at him, sitting there in his Grand Ole Opry suit."

"No. Beyond just White's say-so."

Gload said casually, "It's just bones, Val. Could be anybody."

"There's some identifying feature."

"Don't think so."

"The thing is, he had open-heart surgery. They tell me that every surgeon has a kind of signature way of putting the guy back together. They string wire across his breastbone in a particular way. They're saying they can tell who it is from that."

Gload rocked forward and turned to Millimaki with a bemused smile. "The hell," he said.

"They'll be talking about it this week. Charts, photographs, the whole deal."

"Well, by God, I got to say that's a new one on me."

"Did your lawyer not say anything about it to you?"

"Oh, Jesus Christ, Val. You seen him. That man is three sheets to the wind right this second I guarantee you and we've been out of court for, what is it?"

"An hour. Little more."

"There you go. Right now, drunker than ten Indians. Guaranteed."

"You could petition for different counsel."

"What, a P.D.?" He snorted, smoke erupting from his nostrils. "No, it don't make any difference, Deputy." He cast a sidelong glance at Millimaki. "Ain't you on some kind of ethical thin ice, here, Valentine? Offering legal advice to a felon?"

"Like you said once, we're just talking."

The old killer sat staring at Millimaki's profile. He looked down at the handgun and baton on the deputy's belt and he looked over at the old sandstone jailhouse across the street. He looked for a long time at Millimaki again.

"You look like a goddamn scarecrow, Val, you know that?"

"I've been hearing that a lot lately."

"Your missus not taking care of you? Is that the deal?"

Millimaki turned to stare after a car passing on the street and the old man watched him closely. "Something like that."

"Smoke me, will you please, Deputy?"

When he had smoked for a time Gload said, "Your friend Weldon come a-courting me."

"How do you mean?"

"Wants to be my boyfriend. And he seems pretty intent on stealing your thunder."

Millimaki laughed tiredly. "I don't have any thunder to steal, John."

Gload swung one knee up and clasped it with his manacled hands. He gazed into the rustling dome of greenery overhead. "You got to see all this through that shitbird's eyes. He knows you have the Old Bull's ear and any fool can see he's got some kind of soft spot for you. This turd Wexler, he figures it ought to be him who's the number one son, being as he's been around longer. And him being such a spit-and-polish troop."

Val turned to him. "And how would you come to know all this?"

Gload thrust his chin in the direction of the jail, some hundred feet from where they sat. At that moment the topmost course of stones was awash in rose light. "It's a small town in there, Val."

"Well, in any case, he has been on the force longer than me," Val said. "That doesn't change."

Gload looked once more into the treetops. He was smiling. He said, "It was Weldon's day off today."

"I know. That's why I'm here in the wonderful light of day."

"I got a feeling he spent the day getting his ass full of prickly pear."

Millimaki turned to look at him then. "Why would you have a feeling like that, John?"

"Here's the deal, Valentine. He's got it in his head there's bodies buried all over the place out there, other side of the river. A regular goddamn battlefield. Figures if he can find them he'll be the man of the hour. Detective First Grade. And especially," he said, "if he's the one finds them instead of you."

"How'd he get an idea like that?"

The old man leered and began to shudder imperceptibly. "Ambition is a dangerous thing, Val."

"You shouldn't do that, John, no shit. He could make it bad for you."

The old convict shook his head and his black eyes sparkled. The shuddering became more pronounced and Val thought he might be cold in the orange suit, thin and loose at the seams from a thousand launderings. "Oh, Christ," Gload said. "Oh,

Christ almighty, it would be worth it." He wheezed and water
sprang up in his eyes. "I got this picture in my head of him running up and down them hills with his notebook and a spade.
Running and writing and digging and running some more.
Oh sweet Christ on a crutch." From his pursed lips came a
series of snorts and sharp breaths. Val for a moment thought
he may be beset by a fit. Small tears began to leak from the corners of Gload's eyes. He leaned forward over his knee, shaking
and swinging his great head like a drunken bear. Finally he
wheezed, "Good Lord." He ran the backs of his chained hands
across his eyes and passed his hands over the huge dome of
his head to lay back his hair. It was as close to happy as Val
had ever seen Gload and the old man finally sat gasping and
smiling his strange equine smile. The sun had fallen behind
the courthouse and as they sat on their bench in the long blue
shadow, small birds came and went to nests hidden among the
leafed branches of the elms. Gload turned his attention there
and seemed to address with great seriousness the trees, the sky
beyond circumfused at that hour with sorrel light.

"He'll take your legs out from under you, Val, make no mistake about that."

"I'm not worried about it."

"You oughta be. I'm dead serious about this."

"John, I imagine you've heard the old thing about honor
among thieves. Well, there damn sure is honor among law
enforcement people, too."

"Total bullshit, Valentine. What there is among thieves is
turpitude." He smiled. "Now that right there is a hell of a useful
word."

The old man stared after the sparrows long after they disappeared into the dusk of the leafy canopy. The church bell began

to toll and he looked to Val's watch, which he held up for Gload to read.

"We ought to get on over, John. You'll miss your supper."

Gload dropped his head and seemed to study the tops of his shoes, the thin, dechromed chains around his socks. Presently he said, "In any profession you care to name there are the good and the not so good. Not necessarily good and bad, just good and something short of that. Think about it. For every doctor graduated first in his class there's the one who come out last. Still gets to call himself a doctor, though. Teachers the same. And cops. They ain't all going to be good. There's degrees. It's a simple matter of fact. Fact of life."

"I won't argue that. But it's just that some guys have a different approach than others. Doesn't necessarily make them bad cops."

Gload only smiled. "I'm going to tell you a little story here, Val."

Though he had only just looked at it, Millimaki consulted his watch again. "You're going to miss the meatloaf, John, if we don't go over."

"Couple more minutes."

"About the only thing worth a damn."

The old man looked over at him. "It is a loaf, true enough, but meat? The jury's still out."

"In any case."

The old man sat forward again, his chained hands balanced on his thighs like a man at prayer. Then he sat back against the bench and patted his breast pocket. "Oh, hell," he said. "Would you do me the favor, Val?"

The deputy reached into the breast pocket of Gload's coveralls and removed his smokes and matches. He shook out a cigarette and the old man took it and put it to his lips, his hands in their cuffs paired holding it there as if it were imbued with a great weight. Val struck the match and held it out and the old man moved his head to the flame in a benedictory nod. He drew on it and took it from his mouth with his paired hands. A car went by on the one-way street, teenaged boys already drunk on a beautiful spring evening and they hooted and jeered at the two men, the words tumbling away down the avenue in the rattle of muffler and the blue contrail of exhaust. Faggots. Jail-birds.

"Tough guys," Val said.

"Just rudeness is what it is."

As they watched the car recede, the streetlights began to flutter and shortly the light above the jailhouse door came on. Val said, "I need to get you back."

"A minute, Val," he said. "Humor an old man. Then we can go in." He smoked. "This is something that happened here, oh I guess thirty years ago now." He stopped and smiled, looking as he did again into the green vault overhead. "Thirty years. Jesus Christ. The years do go." And still gazing fondly upward he began to recount a night from his young manhood. It was a time, he said, when he was at the height of his powers. "Not bragging or anything. But I was."

He asked Millimaki if he'd ever told him about his days playing cards in Butte and the deputy said he had. He said there had been a card game with a Chinaman and that he was a real China Chinaman and that he could be barely understood. But poker was a language unto itself and besides it was a game that required little in the way of speech so it didn't matter. The game went long into the night and Gload was well ahead and going along nicely but what caught his eye was the rings on the foreigner's fingers, outsized and electric beneath the low lamp. He recalled that the man was a bit of a dandy, his hair upswept with reeking pomade and gleaming blue-black like a plasticine hat. The Chinaman twisted the rings on his fingers in sequence, a kind of nervous tic, changing the fanned cards from hand to hand, and though Gload could not read the tic as card-tell he read in it the value of the rings.

Gload paused, smiled. "Let me tell you something, Val. It's just like a guy with a full wallet and maybe you didn't know this, but a guy with a full wallet will keep reaching back and putting his hand on it, patting it, like. That's a giveaway. That's just a little tip for you or cheap advice, if you happen to be the guy with the big wallet. So I knew this Chinaman's rings were worth something, by the way he was fooling with them." Val waited, thinking more advice was forthcoming but Gload only sat, erect and staring into the trees and then he continued.

The man was a big bettor and a fair enough cardplayer and he turned the rings constantly, good hand or bad and Gload quickly gave up on that as a way of reading him. His plans began to shape themselves out of the smoke and gloom and they went beyond a game of chance. Chance was not at issue. The night wore on and John Gload from behind his cards studied the man for size and weight, for the fight in him.

Finally he said only that it was a good score. When the game broke up he merely rose and followed the man casually into the alley and killed him. He'd not seen him upright for the entire night and was surprised at how small the man was and how insubstantial, almost like a child in his embrace.

Gload paused and requested another smoke, lit it from the short butt of the previous one and then methodically ground out the stub on the edge of the bench and put it in the breast pocket of his jumpsuit. Millimaki sat mesmerized, found he'd been holding his breath. The old man said, "The hell of it was, I couldn't get them rings off. Sonofabitch Chinaman must have been eating salt by the fistful." He paused, flexed his own thick fingers. "There's some more cheap advice for you, Val—go light on the salt. Salt killed more people than Hitler. Or that other one. The Russian."

With his head down and occasionally turning to regard Millimaki's face, the old man talked on for some time. Val looked over at the jail across the street where already the windows with their latticework of dark bars were burning yellow in the failing light. The small plain birds rose chittering into the harbor of trees.

The old man saw Millimaki look toward the jail and said, "Bear with me just a second. This is going somewheres, I promise."

One of the other players found the luckless Chinaman, sitting spraddle-legged on the alley bricks, the pool of his blood throbbing in the light of a single neon beaconing its lurid color in that dim place. John Gload had held the oriental's throat with one hand against his calling out and when found the little man with his scent of sweet flowers sat with his windpipe crushed and mouth agape as though poised to burst into song. His eyes were wide and they pulsed in the light too with blood pooled at his hands and the great puddle of it between his legs, seeping slowly then from the hole just below his sternum.

The cardplayer had gone into the alleyway to relieve himself but instead stood gaping and vomited down the front of his shirt and ran wordlessly back into the room where the players save two still sat about the table smoking and finishing their whiskey ditches before going home. They stared at the mute

ashen statue pointing toward the dark and they rose and followed him and when the police arrived they found them circling the Chinaman and the Chinaman held his place in the
circle much as he had earlier.

The players spoke with the police in their turn and dispersed,
some to their sleeping wives, some to spare and musty bachelor
rooms two floors above the card room that would seem that
night emptier still.

Among the bills and change in his pocket the Chinese man
had an assortment of pills in a plastic bag and John Gload folded
the bills into his own pockets and emptied the pills with a grunt
of disgust and put the man's fingers with their contrary prizes
in the bag. He went unhurriedly down the cobbles of the dark
alley and kept to the shadows of the awnings and coigns of the
old union halls and by the time he got to his car, no more than
ten minutes had passed since he'd thrown in his last hand.

Through the starless night he drove north with the window
down despite the cold. He stopped at a roadside pull-out at Elk
Park Pass where icy spring water came sluicing from a pipe
into a stone trough and he washed his hands and the knife and
stripped off his trousers and shirt, which were damp yet and
stained with the dead Chinaman's dark arterial blood. He transferred his prizes to the pockets of his fresh pants and then went
lurching like a blind man among pines and brush in the pitch-
dark and buried his clothes under duff and deadfall. At the car
he pared his nails beneath the dome light. He looked into his
red eyes in the rearview mirror for a long moment and palmed
back his hair and pulled once again onto the blacktop. Twice as
he drove he was forced to swerve the Oldsmobile into the ditch
weeds to avoid mule deer standing in the road like lawn statuary with phosphorescent eyes. Gravel rang in the wheelwells.

The radio in that remote country was alive with static but he hummed to the sporadic music nonetheless and the pavement rolled along under his headlights like an endlessly spinning stage prop.

The sun rose red and irresolute in an August sky hazy from distant fires and found John Gload that morning passing through high plains and the buttes of famous western paintings in the near distance began to take shape in roseate geometry, their tabletops afire and from the shadowed slopes birds of prey drifted out over the ripening wheat fields. The highway patrol car passed him going south and he could see its occupant's head swivel and in that instant the light on the cartop began to pulse and the car swung about on the steaming asphalt, through the median in a maelstrom of dust and trash and was behind him, wailing.

He erupted out the passenger side door and through the ditch weeds and took the barbed wire right-of-way fence with one step. The wheat stalks rasped against his legs as he ran but because of the slope of the ground and the difficult purchase of his feet in the soft furrows he seemed to proceed as if in some recurrent nightmare of running and the near-ripe grain flew about him like bees driven from a hive and then he heard the hiss of the first bullet and felt it go by and splat into a rock twenty feet beyond him at the level of his head and so he stopped. He fell to the ground as though in exhaustion and with his head below swaying grain he pulled the Chinaman's fingers from his bloodied pockets, took them from the plastic bag, dug a hole in the soft earth and put them in. He continued forward on his hands and knees, dug another hole for the knife and then he stopped.

"All right, all right," he called. "You got me."

He did not turn but could hear the thud of the patrolman's boots coming across the field and then he could hear the whish-hiss of the wheat stalks on his trousers and then at last the labored breathing.

"Don't move a fucking muscle," the man said. He was breathing very hard. "You sonofabitch."

"You got me," Gload said. "I know I must of been speeding. Didn't know that crate could even go that fast."

"Shit, speeding," the officer wheezed. "My ass speeding."

"Well, I ain't drunk, if that's what it is," Gload said. "I'll walk the line for you. I'm cold sober."

"Shut the fuck up." Gload had taken a kneeling position, still facing the way he had run and he could see ahead of him a small plane in the distance lift off into the perfect blank sky without a sound. It seemed to arise from among the strips of wheat. He felt the barrel-tip press into the base of his skull.

"This is definitely cocked and I'm nervous and I'm breathing real hard," the patrolman said. "And there ain't anybody around for a long long ways to tell how it was you come to have your face splattered on the ground. So don't twitch a eyelash while I put these on you. Put your hands back."

"No, sir," Gload said. "I ain't going to die on account of a speeding ticket."

"Stand up now."

He stood. He turned to face the man then and the sound of the Beechcraft suddenly came to him and above his breathing and the hard breathing of the patrolman he began to hear the whirr of grasshoppers among the amber stems and from the right-of-way fence posts the warble of meadowlarks proclaiming the glory of that day.

"Okay, goddamn it, where's them fingers at?"

"I'd show you but they're cuffed up."

"The Chinaman fingers, asshole."

"Chinaman fingers?"

The plastic bag he'd thrown aside hung atop a clump of wheat stalks and wavered there. The patrolman glanced at it briefly and Gload thought, Blow, wind. He jangled his wrist cuffs and the man looked back to him and the bag filled with air and went skeltering over the grain field like a child's balloon and disappeared.

"Here. Stand out of the way." Gload took two sideways steps in the wheat. "Stand there." The patrolman, a man of perhaps forty-five, began to search about in the wheat, one hand with his service revolver held straight out and his eyes sweeping the ground under their feet. From a distance he might have seemed to be performing some strange ritual dance with the stoic and smiling John Gload for a partner.

"Are they in the car?" he said. "You wouldn't have left them in the car, would you?"

"Officer, you're making my head hurt."

"Shit."

They made their way back through the grain field and at the car the lawman spread Gload on the hot car hood. He sifted through glove compartment papers and with the barrel of his pistol pushed aside crumpled receipts and week-old newspapers lying on the floorboards and atop the Oldsmobile's commodious seats. He took the keys from the ignition and opened the trunk, rummaging for a long while among suitcases and tire chains and an enormous tackle box full of rusted treble snagging hooks and comical oversized lures on wire leaders, raising his head occasionally to scowl at the implacable John Gload. Fifteen minutes later, red-faced and profusely sweating, he leaned against the car's rear quarter panel.

"Goddamn you, Gload," he said, "you didn't eat the sonsof-bitches, did you?"

The old man paused in his telling, smiling, and held up his forgotten cigarette to display its long ash and he sat for a moment with his head to one side listening to the twilight bird-notes from above among the tender leaves.

"Sheriff was so pissed off he sent ten men out there to search that field, up and back, on their goddamn hands and knees and one with a metal detector, I heard. There was a track in the wheat there looked like somebody had drove a truck through by the time me and that highway patrolman got through, so no mistake where we'd been at. Never found nothing." He smiled at Val and shook his head. "That just about damn near killed them. They had to cut me loose."

He sat back then and waited, counting to himself one two three four.

"So what happened to the fingers?" Val said.

Gload smiled. "What do you think?"

"Coyotes? Hell, I don't know. Birds?"

"Val, Val, Val." The old man sighed, as if the task of impart-ing his knowledge were too cumbrous a burden. "It's just like I said. Any line of work you care to name you got what you call degrees of good. Might be the doctor who's the best doctor in the world at what he does but he cheats on his missus. Or say a priest who will sit all night holding the hand of some poor son-ofabitch rotten with the cancer and crying for Jesus and this same man of the cloth pounds down a fifth of Seagram's before lunch. And there are cops who steal, Val. Make no mistake about that."

"The highway patrolman?"

"Give the man a cigar."

"I would doubt that," Val said. "I think that's real unlikely."

Gload went on as if he hadn't heard, his voice distant and quiet with wonderment. "Fucker came within two inches of shooting the top of my head off, then saves my ass out of greed. But can you blame him? Makes probably a thousand a month chasing drunks and scraping people out of burnt cars. He gets a chance to give his girlfriend something nice for once and have a little walking-around money." Gload laughed his croaking laugh. "And nobody out nothing except me and that Chinaman's cat. Bet he puked his guts up, though, getting them rings off. Hell, Val, he earned it right there."

Millimaki shook his head in disbelief.

"Here's my point. Is that if that poor sonofabitch did that for just a little bit of pocket money, don't think for a minute that your pal Wexler wouldn't blindside you for the sake of his so-called career. You know him. He's more than capable of doing that. I just want you to know how things work, Val. I just want you to realize how the world works."

TEN

"A story about a Butte Chinaman and some rings," Millimaki said.

"Oh, Christ, yes."

"Something about fingers and an HP officer."

"Ancient history, Val." The sheriff waved a dismissive hand. "An old story before my time and most likely without merit."

Millimaki experienced a moment of great relief. The prospect of recalling details of Gload's tale of dismemberment and implied departmental failings left him exhausted. Beyond that, he realized with some surprise, he would have felt a sense of betrayal.

"In any event, Deputy, I mostly called you in by way of a follow-up. The last time we spoke there was an issue or issues with your wife. Has that situation improved?"

Millimaki had taken the hard chair opposite the sheriff's desk and he glanced toward the door, beyond which Raylene sat at her vast desk, more formidable at her station there than the ghoulish nightshift bailiff.

"Don't worry about her, Val. Until she finishes her morning crossword she doesn't pay a lick of attention to me. I could be cold as a dead cod in here. When I have my inevitable myocardial infarction I hope it's in the PM."

Together they regarded her back, a broad expanse of garish tropical blooms. Her head beneath its plumed vortex of hair nodded above the page.

"You can close the door if you want, but that usually just sets off her radar."

Millimaki had finished his shift twenty-six hours earlier and had forced himself to stay awake until dark and still he'd hardly slept. The cabin door from its planing now shuddered under the wind and when he'd gotten up and shimmed it tight with two table knives it instead produced a muttering as though words were forming in the outer dark and came encrypted through the moaning gaps. At some point in the very early morning he dreamt again of his mother, her stained lips forming these night sounds into words he could not decipher, though he woke and lay among tangled sheets for an hour trying. He knew he should sleep but the image would not abate. He relented and sat on the edge of his bed watching the new long day paint the windowpanes. Now he sat in front of the cluttered desk blearily regarding his unpolished boots.

"She's staying in town with a friend," he said.

"Ah."

"She's going to stay in town for a while," he said. He looked up, his gaze reaching no higher than the sheriff's chest. "We needed some space. Well, she did anyway."

"Yes. Space. Space is a common theme."

"That's my word. The conversation was a bit more involved than just that."

The sheriff leaned back in his chair. He rested the tips of his index fingers in the slack underside of his jaw. The chair as he imperceptibly rocked emitted a faint feline noise.

"The department is a testing ground for marital Darwinism, Val. This is what we do, one might say what we love to do, but it is frequently opposed to or at least makes difficult the husbanding of marriage. I mean that in the agricultural sense, husbanding. There are additional factors, such as a spouse's profession if there is one outside the home, children from the union. The strongest—" he said.

The younger man had turned his gaze to the streaked single window with its latticework of bars and seemed altogether lost there. The sheriff was unsure if he'd even heard. In any case he was embarrassed to have spoken aloud the philosophy he'd formulated through years of such counseling, years of his own uncounselable grief. He noted in the cruel light the deep furrow that had appeared between Millimaki's brows since he had last seen him and that his pale eyes within their dark grottos were set in a perpetual squint, as if in seeking sense in his world, or succor, he had taken to examining life at the level of mites or atoms.

"You know, Val, my old mother always said that if you make a face long enough it'll be stuck that way."

Millimaki stared into the bright spring day, a long horizontal shadow across his eyes like a man masked before a firing squad. "Does it mean we make a choice?" he said. "Because it seems like it means that if you choose to do your job, I mean to do it right, then your marriage isn't anything more than two people sharing a room for convenience. One gets in bed when the other one goes off to work."

"I'd have to say that that's kind of a harsh view of things," the sheriff said. He slid open a drawer and rummaged about. He came up with his pipe and stuck it cold in the corner of his mouth. "Okay, maybe my theory is just so much happy horseshit, Valentine. Maybe it's just luck. Or chance, whatever you choose to call it. I've seen it a hundred times. Who you marry just goddamn turns out to be some other person after a while. Grows up into somebody else. Not better or worse. Just different."

"You put barley in the drills and six months later it comes up rye."

The sheriff smiled faintly around his pipestem. "Okay, something like that, if we want to keep the agricultural analogies going here." He waited. He dug in the bowl of the pipe with a bent paper clip. Millimaki could see yellow birds, tiny and electric, pinballing from limb to limb in the elms across the street. He thought they might be finches. He watched them through the stained window glass, feeling momentarily as if he were in a cage looking out and the brilliant birds mocked him, flitted about imponderous and free in the wide world. He said, "I guess you get used to the bars after a while."

The sheriff turned to the window, observing as if for the first time the rusty bars there, then looked again at Millimaki. "You could talk to one of our counselors, Val. There's no shame in that."

"I thought if I discharged my weapon. Something like that."

"That's not the only reason we have them."

"I just need some solid sleep."

"We could get something for that. Whatever you need. One phone call."

"Thank you, sir."

"I'm not all that good at pats on the back, Val. I hear it's one of my many failures. But you're a good officer. And I've not seen anyone better with a dog. Not since I've been here." He took the pipe from his mouth and examined the bowl thoughtfully then set it on the desk. "In many ways you remind me of me."

"And you're still married."

"Yes. Well. Again and still."

Millimaki turned from the window and looked at him. "I didn't know that."

"It was a long time ago, Val. Don't extrapolate anything from that."

A car passed on the street below. In the ensuing quiet only the rhythmical mewing of the sheriff's chair. Finally he said, "Was Teagarden here when you started? I can't recall."

"No, sir. I remember hearing the name."

"Ed Teagarden—married thirty-two years, the whole time he was on the force. Nice woman. Good woman. And smart." He stopped abruptly then, remembering, and began to busy himself with the seeming unfathomable jumble atop his desk. His glasses were revealed and he put them on and looked down. He took them off and examined them as if they might be glasses left behind by someone else and then set them on the desk again.

"Yes, sir. That's it? He was the only one?"

"No, hell." The sheriff scanned the desk as if an answer might appear there, among the envelopes of overnight mail and yellow and red carbons and triplicate forms requiring his signature a thick dossier on the long and happily married men who had served under him. "Well, the only one comes to mind. There must have been more. I'm sure of it."

"Dobek?"

"Voyle Dobek. Wedded four times that I'm aware of. But he's Dobek. He is not representative."

Millimaki went out of the office, his feet heavy and his head dull. As he passed Raylene's desk he paused and seemed to study with great concern the floor beneath his feet. The secretary glanced up at him from her folded paper and after a moment looked up at him again and laid aside her pencil. "Can I help you, Deputy?"

Millimaki said, "Is it too early for a goldfinch?"

ELEVEN

They tracked him along a dry watercourse in country that had been mapped for a hundred years but, like the charts of ancient seas with their dragons and monstrous waves, its details were little more than conjectural. There was in some years grass enough for cattle but the getting them in and bringing them out of such broken and waterless territory proved an enterprise of insufficient profit. Cattle wild as elk were said to live there, their numbers checked now by big cats and spectral wolves, drought and blizzard.

The ground underfoot was hot and the very air seemed to shudder in the heat and everywhere was the hiss and crackle of grasshoppers. "You got a lot of heart for the old crazy man they say you are," Millimaki said. The dog stopped to look back at him, his tongue lolling. They had already walked five miles and he could see ahead for nearly another mile into the empty country. A hawk far to the north circled above the invisible lake. A sparrow on a sage limb dazed by heat. The dog sniffed briefly at a cow dead some two or three years, disarticulated by flash flood or scavengers and it looked to have fallen from the sky and burst apart. A tatter of red hide lay across the cage of ribs like parchment.

In pursuit of God knows what the old man had walked into that bleak quarter in the third week in July from a scorched and dust-blown campsite on the shore of Fort Peck Reservoir. His family searched for hours, until they feared becoming lost themselves in the utter dark, and the following late morning Valentine Millimaki arrived, having driven straight into the sunrise for three and a half hours after his interminable graveyard shift. He stood beside the exploded Hereford at seven-thirty in the evening and was himself beginning to suffer from lack of water and sleep.

"I set him up with a pole and a chair and a gob of worms and then we took the boat out," the man said. "We weren't gone but half an hour and he's nowheres. Must of started walking soon as we started the goddamn motor."

"So you were gone about a half an hour."

"Something like that."

Val looked to the man's wife for confirmation.

"I wish you wouldn't swear right at this time," she said to her husband. She turned to Millimaki. "It could of been an hour," she said. "Up to an hour."

"Might of been," the man said. "It was like somebody just called him away to supper. Pole laying right there next to the chair with the line still out. It was all snagged up by the time we got back. I had to bust it off."

The missing man's daughter stood with her husband near the

lakeshore, very slender and pale, holding herself quite still as if, like gossamer or a clutch of down, she might come apart in the merest movement of summer air. Both of them from their frantic pursuit of hunch and shadows among the hills and along the beach were sunburned a terrifying red. She said, "It's like a switch you throw." The irises of her eyes were the color of sapphires and seemed to Millimaki about to liquefy, integuments too frail to restrain such pain. She studied the infinity of sky beyond his head. "He'd be so good and normal, calling me by my right, real name and even the kids' names and then it's like a switch. He'd get this terrible look on his face like who was this stranger in his house trying to make him eat poison food. That's how it was."

"We fed him good," the man offered.

"That's not what I'm telling him," she said.

"I know it isn't."

"Then just don't say anything."

She wept openly then, hugging herself like someone standing in a cold place. "Oh, Daddy." Her husband seemed not to know how to comfort her, his hand wavering in the air above her head in a gesture of blessing and finally he merely rested it on the back of her sunburned neck.

Shortly and with a visible effort she composed herself. "He'd say he heard her calling, say, 'There's Clara,' and up he'd get, didn't matter from where. From the dinner table, wherever. In church. Up he'd get and go off."

She stood with her red arms at her waist, the man's hand on her neck. Beyond them the two children sat in the dirt in their bathing suits disconsolately batting an inflatable ball between them. The boy wore thick glasses and he looked up at Millimaki with enormous magnified eyes.

"So I know where he went," the woman said. Millimaki looked at her and her husband looked away. "He's gone out there looking for Mother," she said. "She's been gone three years and he's out there looking for her in the hills."

Tom sat at heel watching the ball and when the woman began to wail he turned to her, cocking his head side to side.

"I'm sorry," Val said. The couple stood before him, the water beyond their backs as flat and reflective as plate glass. "Can you tell me what he was wearing?"

"Ain't like there's anybody else out there to confuse him with," the man said.

Val looked up at him. Far out in the dazzling lake a floating island of ethereal blue pines and sage frissoned in the heat haze—a realm of myth as axiomatic as the ground under him and then that quickly it was gone.

"Colors," he said. "I like to know what colors to look for."

"T-shirt and these brown pants he always wore," the man said. "Them khaki pants, same as he wore to work for thirty years, sweeping at the school." He shook his head. "Some whatchamacall pull-on type shoes 'cause he couldn't work the laces no more. Is that sound about right, Honey?"

The woman wiped at her eye with the back of her wrist. "A white T-shirt," she said. "And a cap. I put a cap on his head when we left, for the sun. Just a ball cap of Jamie's. I don't know what was on it. It was black, I guess."

The boy looked over, pouting. "It was NASCAR and it was my favorite and now it's gone."

The man turned to him. "Don't you start that again."

"'S true, though."

"What color, son?" Val said.

"Purple and yellow and red with 26 on it." He stared at the dog. "Can he find it? Can Whatever-His-Name-Is find it for me?"

"He's Tom. He'll give it a heck of a try."

"Just a white T-shirt," the woman said. "And the cap and the pants."

"All right."

Heat waves shimmered up from the camp trailer, the blue tarp canopied over the doorway casting a rhombus of meager shade. Two cinder blocks secured it atop the trailer and through the grommet holes two poles held it bellied over the dirt where spavined lawn chairs had been placed.

"I'd like some more water for the dog, and could you get a piece of your father's clothes for me? A shirt or pants, something like that. It'll help the dog getting started."

Val went to the truck and began provisioning himself for the long day. The man came over, holding a pale blue windbreaker that had been his father-in-law's.

"Sorry for what I said. It's been pretty tough around here. She's blaming me for it. I know she don't mean it but she is."

"Don't worry about it," Val said.

"I looked everywhere." He gazed out over the flat surface of the lake. "Could he be out there? He might of just waded out in the lake and that was it."

"Could have," Millimaki said. "But Tom didn't show any interest there. Sounds like he went walking. Pretty common with Alzheimer's. They just walk and walk."

"Don't I know it." The man stood awkwardly with his huge laborer's hands buried in the pockets of jeans that had apparently been sheared off rudely at the knee with a knife or an ax. The tops of his gnarled feet were crimson and peeling. "Sometimes he just pissed in his pants," he said. His voice cracked. "Sitting there. My wife changes him like a baby."

"You did good," the deputy said. "You did all you could."

"I might go along with you."

"No. Stay with your family. Tom anyway gets all flummoxed if he's got to keep an eye on more than one."

"All right. But ain't there anything you want me to do?"

"If I don't come back call out a sheriff and his dog."

"Oh, hell." The man took off his hat and ran his rough fingers through his hair and regarded the vast country sprawled behind them.

"I'm kidding," Val said. "But you might get a good fire going once it gets dark and keep it going. Should be able to see it from a long ways off. Maybe get your missus to sit out there with you. Give her something else to think about."

He adjusted the canteens on his belt and called the dog to heel and began to walk away when the man called after him. "Listen, I know you're thinking what could he catch out of there." He waved behind him at the murky lake just then the color of calcimine under the featureless sky. The water hissed softly on the graveled shingle. "I just wanted him to have something to do. Anyways, he might of tied into a carp or a goldeneye, something to tug on the line at least."

After they set out the shepherd was immediately drawn to a streambed entering from the south and the going in that direction was slow: deep troughs and cutbanks and a twisted wrack of weathered plank and post and deadfall from some headland flood of the previous spring. Queer rocks lay atop the dirt as smooth and round as Jurassic eggs, and pinecones tumbled and abraded by the torrent lay all about like spined sea creatures of a past age. Grasshoppers wheeled up before them and rattled off into the weeds and sage.

They walked on for some time, the dog working back and forth across the wash. Juniper and pine appeared atop the banks, the larger trees displaying weeping blazes where porcupine teeth had been at work. Roots snaked exposed over the parched ground, encircling stones as though to squeeze sustenance from them. Sandstone scarps filigreed with fossil fish and shells projected atop the cutbanks like the pulpits of sailing ships and everywhere startling columns of the ancient stone wind-carved and pocked like sculpture from a fever dream.

Atop a small rise an hour later they came upon a low homestead cabin of notched and squared-off logs and the dog raised his nose and angled toward it. A flicker of hope invigorated Millimaki and he jogged up the bank on which the cabin stood, the black rectangle of its doorway promising the only substantial shade for miles in any direction. They had not seen where the man had spent the night and Millimaki prayed he might be resting his old bones in the cabin's cool interior.

But he was not. Tom whined and circled in the dusty dark and Millimaki could see in the pale dirt, among tracks of pack rats and skunk and badger, the man's shoe prints trod in a circle no larger than a barrel lid. He had stood there turning and turning about for some time and had at last gone out into the bright alien world again.

It was very quiet there. Tom lay in the dirt panting. The cabin door was stove in, hanging atilt from a hinge fashioned from a boot sole and Millimaki, dizzy and half-blind in the sudden twilight, stood looking back the way they'd come. It was a strangely resolute course for a man who'd had difficulty navigating the hallways of his daughter's home, a track not at all like the zags and insensate back-loops of so many of the poor souls he'd pursued over the years who'd wandered crazed or hypothermic through deadfall or thigh-deep in freezing creeks or like maddened fugitives scaled sheer cliffs, leaving bloody fingernails wedged among the fissures. The frightened woman at the campsite had said her father had gone off in search of his dead wife and perhaps she was right. He seemed to be drawn by something, and as Millimaki stood atop prints of the old man's cheap shoes, the word "quest" came into his bleary head. Quest, he thought. What the hell, I'm losing it.

He had not slept in more than twenty hours, and fatigue crept down his bones in a slow paralysis. He imagined the old janitor himself standing there earlier, the adze scars on the logs transubstantiating into some long-ago wallpaper pattern his wife had chosen for their home. Where swallows flitted now among the bellied pine poles of the ceiling he heard the twitter of his children from their bedrooms. And then her voice again. It had brought him here but now moved on, a faint and musical rendering of his name on the wind and in the branches of the trees.

Shadows like viscous ink slid down the coulee sides and gave sinister shape to the sandstone totems and crags accoutered with high-water jetsam and there were shapes enough among them to populate any dream or nightmare, even in a sound mind. Box elder trees with their eveningtime shadows came to resemble groping mandrake creatures, and raptors planing high overhead gave voice to them, and the roots of the dark pines lay atop the rutted ground like vipers.

The day was far advanced when Millimaki and the dog stood among the bones of the ill-starred Hereford. He stared at the bleached jumble about his feet as if it might be an augury he was meant to decipher but in his diminished state he could hardly unriddle the mystery of his own compass. He was astounded the man, eighty-six years old, could have come so far in such country, driven it seemed by a love that had endured fifty years to pursue glimpse and figment, the specter of his wife beckoning at each bend of the baking streambed. Or was it that, like Tom, he merely followed the scent on the breeze of lilac or rosewater or the redolence of the soap that for two thousand nights she'd used before she came to lie beside him in their bed. Such feelings for Millimaki were as cold and remote as an expired star and he was better able to conjure images of the old man's wife than of his own, grown faceless and undefined in the mere weeks since she'd abandoned him.

Millimaki rubbed at his afflicted eyes and consulted his watch. When he stared up and addressed the sky, gone lavender at the late hour, his tongue felt thick. "Where in the Christ are you, old man?"

The dog Tom at that moment began to whine, circling near a ravelment of roots and deadfall piled up by a long-ago flood; it looked like the den of some Pleistocene rodent. The grandson's cap lay in the dirt and the ground was scuffed and gouged by the man's shoes as though he had struggled there with a phantom.

The dog's tail began to wag furiously and he bolted away, pink tongue hanging long from his mouth. He ran ahead and waited for Millimaki and ran again. After nearly a mile of this, the deputy saw a snatch of white far ahead—a color, save for bones, absent in all the dun and darkening landscape. He did not trust his eyes. He shambled the last short way on feet heavy as bricks.

A magpie stood on the man's very back, pulling at the fabric of his shirt almost as if it merely wanted to wake him from his sleep. It flew on their approach and from a juniper branch assailed the dog with splenetic speech so nearly human the dog stood and stared. The man lay on his face and seemed to have fallen head-long as though pushed from behind. Every inch of his exposed pale skin was terribly burned and shot with blisters and he lay in the dirt slowly baking.

He had been bitten by a snake high in the groin, his left leg swollen horrifically so that the fabric of his trousers was stretched tight and discolored by the thin fluid seeping from the wound. The snake was a prairie rattler probably five feet long and thick as bridge cable and wound around the old man's arm like strange Egyptian bijouterie. It seemed in his confusion and rage he had grabbed the snake behind the head and just hung on. The dog sniffed at him and warily sniffed the snake and finally merely sat. Val took out his small camera from the fanny pack he wore and circled, taking his pictures of the ground and the man in his repose and close pictures of the wound in the bloated leg. He snapped a frame of the snake locked in the man's grip, an image he'd later think seemed strangely mild and as unthreatening as a sock puppet, with its extended tongue a thin filament dry as a strip of felt. At last he sat beside the dog, in the cup of his hand giving him long drinks of water from one of the canteens. He'd saved it for the old man but now he and the dog drank deeply. As the poison moved in his veins, the man with the snake in his grip plodded up the narrow watercourse for nearly a mile toward the timbered headland above, which now, as Millimaki sat regarding his rigid shape, sent down from its slopes on the breeze a perfumery of sage and juniper and pine. Millimaki was very tired and sat looking up at the bluff and at the trees silhouetted on a sudden pearl light. Presently he rose and moved to the corpse and turned it over. It was a wooden thing, a carving attired with a workman's costume and a thespian's mask of awe, of wonderment, eyes agape and painted the same heart-rending blue as his daughter's.

Shadows lay long across the ground and stars began to materialize and from the uplands stretching off toward the Judith River Millimaki heard the first tentative yawps of coyotes. He closed his eyes and rested his forehead on his knees. The dog slept. The old man slumbered rigidly near his feet.

And then he saw her, standing young and fresh and a little impatiently on the bluff, the wind moving her hair. She waited and soon her knight, this haggard warrior—burner of trash, sweeper of floors—went to her. And there was nothing else but her, not the crushing sorrow, not the sun that baked his skin or the pain in his leg or the vile writhing thing around his arm. His steps were light and he gained the top of the hill with scarcely a breath and they stood together on that palisade gazing out over the green and perfect flowering prairielands of their life. In his dream Millimaki watched as Tom scrabbled up the rocky slope and circled whimpering and at last lost the scent he'd followed as it spiraled into the troposphere like a wisp of smoke.

Millimaki woke and sat looking fondly at the dark terrible shape and then put his head on his knees once more as the blue dusk settled over him with the whisper of bees. Tom came to nuzzle him, staring into his face with sad moist eyes and finally lay down beside his feet. A three-quarter moon ascended above the hills and all was silvery light. Millimaki was reluctant to leave the old gentleman's company.

He held the dog by the collar and stood for a long time in the dark. Driftwood in the fire snapped with the sound of breaking bones. When he approached, the man and his wife sat stupefied before the flames and they stared at Millimaki wide eyed and amazed as though he were the conjurement of their bleak thoughts, a figure portioned out from the darkness itself. Beyond them the lake was a sheet of quicksilver, so flat and calm Millimaki could make out gulls or ducks arrayed on its surface hundreds of yards out and could as well have been a fleet of ships at anchor.

"God almighty, you scared us, Deputy."

Millimaki stood in the circle of light. "Could I get a drink of water for Tom?"

The family had drug up a cottonwood log from the lake that had been worn white and smooth as a great tusk and he stepped over it and sat. The dog disappeared into the dark and could be heard lapping endlessly at the lake edge. The man set the bowl down next to Millimaki.

"Anyways, in case he wants it," he said. He handed Millimaki a long-necked beer, its sides pearled with dew. Millimaki felt something in his pocket and he fished out the boy's cap and set it on the log beside him.

The woman had not taken her eyes from him as he came up and sat and she said at last, "He's dead out there, isn't he?"

Millimaki regarded the shifting coals. "Yes, he is," he said. "I'm sorry."

"I knew it, anyways," she said. "It's all right. It's what he wanted."

"He was a strong man. You didn't tell me that," Millimaki said blearily. "He went a long ways." The heat and lack of sleep and general unnamed sadness lay atop him like a succubus. He sat with his forearms on his knees and was surprised to find a bottle in his hand. He couldn't bring himself to tell them about the snake and it seemed sufficient tonight that they picture their father intact and comfortably asleep under the cosseting sky. Almost to himself he said, "I can't believe how far he went. In that heat." He shook his head. "Might have been seven miles. More maybe. Eight or nine."

"He's done that a couple of times back at home," the husband said. "One time they found him out by the airport, better than twelve miles from the house."

"Anyways, it's what he wanted." The old man's daughter wore a thin sweater thrown over her shoulders and she pulled it tighter around her. "He's with Mother now."

The man sat sunk in a canvas camp chair, a beer bottle dangling from his hand while he stared back at the sputtering coals. "Why couldn't he of just died in his chair at home," he said. He shook his head. "To go out there in that." He tipped his bottle vaguely toward the Breaks, the headlands and blunt pines rumored against a backdrop of outrageous starfields. "It's awful. It's undignified is what it is."

"I won't hear that," his wife said. "Lawrence, I won't hear it."

"Well."

"It's not true." She was quiet for a long while. The fire welled brightly as a breeze rose up, collapsing wood sending up a rosary of brilliant embers. A luminous cloud lay across the moon.

"He was on a search is what I believe." The woman paused,

her face in the firelight ruddled and exaggerated as a native mask. "A kind of search. I can't think of the word."

Millimaki did not look up. He spoke almost as if from a dream. "A quest," he said.

"Well, yes." She looked at him in surprise. "That's exactly the word. A quest. He was. He's been on a quest for Mother since she died. Far as he was concerned, she was somewheres just out of sight, just around the next corner. And don't look at me like that. Do you have to look at me that way?"

Her husband said, "I wasn't looking any way."

"I know that look." Her voice quavered. "I know that look, Lawrence."

The man stared at her for a long moment. The wind passed over them and Millimaki imagined it bringing the old man's scent out across all the broken implacable country, to all the hunger that resided there and the wind blew the woman's pale hair across her mouth and sent a chill down her frame. She was still, in middle age, as slender as a girl.

The man cast his eyes sidelong to look at Millimaki. "Deputy," he said, "don't you have someone waiting on you? You must want to bust out of here and get home."

Enthralled by the pulsing coals and numb with fatigue, Millimaki registered the words slowly. Both of them watched him. The wind blew. Their shadows loomed and collapsed and loomed again on the ground beyond them.

"My wife," he said stupidly, "she—"

"That's right," the man said. "Go on. You don't need to wait on us. You go on and be with her."

With that he set his bottle down carefully next to his feet and stood up. Millimaki watched him. He circled out into the dark and reappeared behind his wife, his face red and demonic in the upflare of the fire and his hard hands aglow and he wrapped his arms around his wife's shoulders as tenderly as if he were trying to contain a cloud. She reached up and held his forearms in her small hands and began to softly cry. "Oh, he was, Lawrence. He was."

The wind swept down and the old man's daughter wept, repeating, like an affirmation of her father's simple life, "Oh, he was, he was, he was."

TWELVE

"I suppose I ought to mention this one other thing, though it don't amount to any mystery or anything. When I was a young buck in Deer Lodge I had to get a guy who was after me. They never could prove who it was, though I had to do a two-week haul in Siberia East because they knew more or less what was going on and they figured it was me. There was a corner by the cellhouse, the only place the towers couldn't see and I got this guy over there. There was a kind of outdoor urinal there that you maybe've seen if you've been there. A piss trough. Lot of shit went down there, guys trading dope and getting it on with one another and shit like that and I figured he'd come over when I was taking a piss just to have a look and of course he did, hissing terrible awful things to a boy. Yeah, that was the deal. You could find out easy enough I guess, if you cared. I don't remember his name but he was a fat dago fairy from Butte, Montana, and he deserved what he got. It was that I didn't have no choice is why I don't mention it much and he come over and I put a shiv up under his fat gut and just pulled it upwards hard as I could and he fell down hard with his blue guts spilt out on the stones like a steer you'd butcher. And then I went and pissed the blood off my hands and walked away and that was that.

"I'm tired now, Val. There wasn't anything more to it than that. Good night."

THIRTEEN

He held the crude map in his hands and surveyed the country below him. He looked at the page then turned it half around and looked again. It was like a child's drawing. The old criminal had drawn horseshoes to approximate the upper and lower dams and inverted Us with strange diacritical marks to indicate hills with their sparse native vegetation. He had incised thick black lines apparently with the paper poised on his knee because in places the paper was torn through, these meant to represent coulees, which converged like veins into a river replete with tiny waves and gulls. To Wexler finally it looked like an idiot's rendering of a storybook land. The old man had drawn in trees and a series of inverted Vs that might have been distant mountains by which to orient oneself, and finally in various places he had marked a number of bold Xs. Wexler stared all around. He turned the pages once more.

By the time he returned to his car the sun was nearly down.

He sat on the bumper, with a stick chiseling mud from the soles of his boots. When he was done he took the old man's map and oriented it and sat looking up into the coulees he'd walked, which at that late hour lay in cool blue shadow. Beyond the bluff tops he could see the peaks of the Highwoods purple and insubstantial in the distance as a reef of summer storm cloud.

With the folding entrenching tool he'd dug three holes that day that had yielded nothing but rocks and the ironlike roots of sagebrush and one ancient bone that may have been the pinbone of a cow or buffalo. Wexler had examined it for some time and had laid it alongside his own thighbone and finally had thrown it away in disgust. Now, sitting at his car, he studied the maps once more in the failing light and looked to the north again and finally balled up the pages and threw them into the ditch weeds.

"Goddamn you, old man," he said. He seemed to address the papers now fluttering like wounded birds in a snarl of mullein and hemlock. "If you're screwing me around I swear to God I'll make your hayseed boyfriend wish he'd never left the farm."

Walking in a daze, Millimaki followed the old man as he trundled slowly down the corridor, his shadow on the waxed concrete, giant and dwarf, as he passed beneath the buzzing overheads. From the cells some of the men called to him. Gload went along as if he were walking alone in his orchard and the voices of the inmates were to him less consequential than the trill of birds in the apple trees. They'd just returned from the infirmary after Gload had complained of chest pains and dizziness and the caged men behind the safety of their bars called him piker and scammer and goldbrick. Millimaki turned to one man whose narrow head nearly fit between the bars where he stood hissing a disjointed litany of obscenities.

"One more word and it's lights out, right now," Millimaki said. "Get back to your cot or I'll call for Dobek."

The man hissed a long "muthafucka." Millimaki swung his baton viciously and hit the bars above the man's head. "Get back to your goddamn cot, Murphy, or I swear to Christ I'll come in there and crush your head myself." He had raised the club again, his hand tingling and aflame and felt in that incandescent moment if the face appeared at the bars he could turn bone to gruel. But the man whined and slunk soundlessly into the shadows and could be heard for many minutes in conversation with himself there.

Gload stood before his cell door and waited for Val to turn the key in the lock and he went in without a word, though in passing he eyed the younger man with a bemused expression that furrowed his immense forehead. Millimaki heard him sit in his chair, saw the match flame erupt in the gloom.

"Would you like to talk about it, Val?" he said.

Millimaki with the keys in his hand stood outside the door. The men had settled down in their cells, but for Murphy, who addressed the dark recesses intimately in two separate voices, two separate selves. His moist and horrible lips made the sound of dripping water.

"Did you say something, John?"

"I said you might want to get it off your chest, whatever it is that's eating on you."

"It's late, John. What don't you get some sleep? That's probably all that's wrong with you."

"That ain't going to happen. I can feel it. Not tonight it ain't." He lit another cigarette and his mask appeared briefly hovering in the dark. "Take your walk, Valentine. I'll be here should you feel the need to talk."

Millimaki made his rounds. The jailer, who with every long week seemed to become more like the statue of some Old Testament god, gazed down from atop his platform with hollow eyes, his face carved from yellow stone by indifferent hands and deeply shadowed from the sallow overhead globelight. No longer sure when he was awake or when he slept, Millimaki had quit trying to speak to him and so sat silently filling in the night's required forms and eating an apple from his simple lunch. A soft rain fell and muted the church bells tolling the three o'clock hour, and the lacquered street beyond the jailhouse door reflected the streetlight's purple albedo and the lights of the infrequent passing cars. The phone rang and he turned to watch the jailer, willing him to nod and hold up the receiver toward him. The rain did not matter nor the hour. He would go to her then or anytime and pack her things into the truck to bring her home. The jailer from his imperious elevated seat would say to him, "It's your wife, Millimaki," and he'd go out under the weeping eaves and pass under the streetlamp. He could see himself doing it, getting up from his desk and opening the door to the slow gong, gong, gong, and feeling the cool kiss of mist on his face.

But the jailer only leered from his seat and half turned away from Millimaki for privacy and so he went through the sally gate and down the corridor of cells.

As if because he was cursed to sleeplessness, John Gload had become expert in the nuances of sleep. Sporadically, in stretches of months, sometimes years, he'd had time to decipher the night's minute tickings, the folds and creases of it while caged men near him slept, twitching or writhing in unconsciousness while their breath rifled in and out through constricted throats and nostrils that had been malformed in fights and those still capable expiating their sins in the confessionals of dreamland. For some the commodious limits of the cell became in nightmare the close configuration of their own coffins and they battled their rough blankets as though they were the winding clothes they'd worn to the grave and there were others who relived in prurient languor trysts with women gagged with their own hosiery or mute children or other weaker men waylaid in the showers of a recurring incarceration and John Gload read in these moans and sighs, in the wet and strangled sounds in their mouths, the sins of flesh duplicated in their slumbering. Dead people paraded through Gload's dreams, too, but he was untroubled by them and though they were his victims and wore rubious scars, they seemed no more strange to him than the random beings populating any man's dreams.

"They're all asleep, Val," the old man said.

Millimaki paused, his shadow leaning to merge with the dark of Gload's cell.

"Why not pull up your chair, Deptee?"

Gload had come to the bars from his chair and his hands dangled atop the door's horizontal cross member, the cigarette smoldering at his stained knuckle. He stood with his sloping equine forehead pressed to the bars. Rarely in their talks had he come forward from the gloom and Millimaki had long since grown accustomed to speaking to a voice in the dark and hearing one issue from the dark and their relationship because of that had taken on the aspect of priest and confessor, the roles unfixed and seeming to change by the minute. The old man stood staring at the ember of his cigarette, waiting.

"Why not sit for a bit?"

Millimaki stood. He listened. Lights flared in the street-level window, and tires on the wet pavement beyond made a brief adder's hiss. He turned and found his chair against the corridor wall where for the first time he noted the paint peeling in long yellow skeins and it lay on the floor like molted skins and the walls wept a drapery of griseous stains under every window where water had breached the rotting jambs. He brought the chair forward and sat heavily.

"This new Murphy guy seems to of pushed some kind of button on you," Gload said.

Millimaki ran his hand through his hair and massaged a spot at the base of his skull. "He just happened to be within reach. I lost my cool."

"I wouldn't give it a second thought, Val. He's a bad one."

"Not many wind up here for their good Christian deeds."

The old man smiled. "You're right, Valentine. But there's bad and then there's crazy. With your crazies like this Murphy you lose the whole benefit of knowing what they might do next. I've walked a wide circle around his type my whole life."

"And it's served you well."

Gload sat frozen with the cigarette halfway to his lips. "Your point being that I'm in this place and so is he and so what have I gained."

With the heels of his hands Millimaki ground at his eye sockets and he sighed. "I'm sorry, John. I'm not much in the way of company tonight."

"I hear you had a walk in the toolies with your dog. Is that the problem?"

"Like you said, it's a small town in here."

"Nobody has nothing to do but talk, Val. Myself I mostly listen."

"Not much of what these guys say would seem too interesting."

"So you found another one cold and stiff. You're on a bum run of luck, Valentine. But that will change."

"I keep hearing that."

Gload stood with his arms through the bars. When he pulled his head back to bring the burning cigarette to his lips, two faint outlines of the bars were pressed onto his forehead.

"You haven't had a lot to say these days, Deputy. What's on your mind?"

"Very little, John. Sleep. Sleep is on my mind."

"You could try my little trick."

"It's three in the morning and you're standing here talking to me. Not a particularly good advertisement for it."

"Sometimes," Gload said. "Sometimes." With his Camel clinched between knuckles he sat hingeing his wrist up and back, watching in the gloom the tiny bolide of its burning tip. "Tonight I thought you might want to talk."

"So you stayed up to talk to me."

"I'm sorry that after what we been through you'd be so surprised by that." He blew his smoke toward the overhead lights and watched it vanish. "Yes, Deputy, I stayed up to talk to you."

It was out of his mouth before he'd time to consider it and in the intervening short moment of silence afterward he felt ridiculous. "It's my wife."

Gload received the news with gravity. He ground out his cigarette in the tin can and the chair's legs chirped as he inched it closer to the bars and he composed his hands in his lap like a man at prayer. "You sorta had that look," he said.

"She's gone to stay in town with a girlfriend. I hardly saw her before. Now I never do."

"That's no way to carry on a relationship. If I was to add up the days I was gone while I was with Francie I'd say it was damn near two of the five years. I don't recommend it."

"Francie. That's your wife?"

"Not wife, exactly."

"What then?"

There came a long pause during which the sounds of the old building seemed to insinuate themselves overloud like crickets on an August evening. Fans whirred somewhere far away in its mechanical heart and its breath came fusty and dry from the ductwork. Gload's voice when he finally spoke was scarcely louder than the indifferent mutterings of the air conditioner.

"You asked me once before if she was my wife and I never answered you which was rude and I apologize. But I hadn't ever the need to describe her to anybody which you'll think is kind of peculiar but I guess that tells you something about how we lived. Not exactly out in the public eye much, so to speak."

"So would you say 'girlfriend' then? Or your 'Old Lady'?"

"Old Lady," he snorted. "Gah. I hate that. Sounds like some of that bullshit biker talk." He paused to draw on his smoke and exhale into the light. "No, and I'm too goddamn old for 'girl-friend.' So I guess 'wife' is the best one. It's how I feel about her anyways."

"And she left you."

"What I said was—" What he'd said was she was gone and that was a different thing entirely. But from his innominate shadows he could read in the young man's eyes—insomniacal and familiar, so much like those that regarded him in the scarred and untrue polished metal of his cell's mirror—a need for the comfort bestowed by mutual anguish.

"Yes she did," Gload said and thought, My little Francie. "She left me for something better."

Millimaki nodded. Like two men at a campfire they sat listening to the night sounds in the dark beyond their strange violet circle of light. Millimaki had closed his eyes and soon his head began to bob as if the bones in his neck had turned to jelly. He lurched upright, his eyes wild. The old man had been watching him solemnly.

"Shit," Millimaki said. "I need to get up and get moving before I crap out right here."

In his weariness Millimaki in rising placed a hand on the flat horizontal bar of John Gload's cell and the old man reached and laid his enormous paw over it. Val stared at the great hairy thing, white and thick and heavy, and made no move to pull away. The old man left it there for a moment and then it was gone into shadow. It was the first human contact Millimaki had experienced in weeks. The last person he'd touched—the old janitor wandering in the badlands in search of his young bride—had been made of oak.

Gload sat back. "I feel like I want to tell you this one thing, Valentine. Sit down. Sit for just a minute."

Millimaki hesitated briefly. He cast his gaze to the right where the nicked and rusty bars on the cells seemed to diminish infinitely like notches numerating the dead. The caged men behind them slept on.

When the deputy had taken his chair, Gload said, "One thing I always did, Val, was to live my life. It wasn't a particularly interesting life but it was on my terms. Now in here I'm just living it out."

"I'm not sure what you mean."

"Now it's just waiting. It's only a life technically because you're breathing in and out. Putting in the time until you clock out." He brought forward his chair with a squawk yet again and slid his bean can beside his foot.

"I was in this little town once some years ago over east of here and every day I'd walk past this place for old people. Hospital for old people. A whatyacallit—old folks' home?"

"Nursing home?"

"I don't know. Whatever they call it these days. But with this line of people sitting in their chairs or wheelchairs just looking out. Me walking by was the best part of their day. A week I went by there every morning on the way for a paper up the street and back and I seen them there, heads moved all of a piece to follow me just like cattle. They were just living it out, you see what I mean, Val? Waiting it out. And one day I just turned and went in. They were sitting there, didn't look at me at all because it was out the window where the world was. Didn't even turn their heads. They were nothing but sticks in clothes. Blankets on their laps, hair standing up all which-way. I just stood there. Pretty soon I folded the paper and put it in my back pocket. I thought that in about half a minute I could snap their necks one two three down the line and then this pogue comes in eating a chicken leg in his dirty white jacket and says can I help you and then that was that."

Millimaki studied the old man or rather studied the space he knew him to occupy in the dark and then from that space smoke rolled into the artificial light.

"You're serious."

"Serious as God." Through the bars a hand appeared, corpse-white in the light and brutal, two fingers held a fraction of an inch apart. It was not at all the same warm thing that had rested on his own hand a few short minutes before. "That fucking close," he said. "I was fixing to do it and I could of. Don't think I couldn't."

"An act of kindness, then?" Millimaki said.

"In that case I believe it was mostly just impatience on my part."

"Those people had memories at least. To go back to."

"They had shit, Valentine." Gload tapped a finger twice above his pendulous ear. "There was nothing upstairs but oatmeal." He sat back into shadow and was quiet a long while. The tube lights throbbed and hissed. Millimaki waited. "But it would of been a kindness, Val, yes indeed. Or a blessing, some might call it, who believe in such things. Like you. Didn't you not tell me once you were a mackerel snapper?"

"I was raised that way. Pretty sure I never mentioned it though."

Gload waved away the remark, his hand winking into the light and gone again. "Anyways, you have to see what I'm getting at."

"I'm tired, John. Maybe you could help me see your point."

"Like people at the end of the line. Like some of the folks you find, Valentine. They would of been better off dead, is my point."

On the thin mattress Gload lay atop was a cartography of a thousand stains and there were more stains and thin fissures like the veins in a leaf on the ceiling above his head in the muddled dark. Across his counterfeit heaven, visions of Francie came and went like the random flares of headlights through the high corridor windows. As if he looked at her again through the old imperfect panes of their house or one washed with rain, her

face was blurred. But her singing was in his ears, her voice calling his name as if it were a chant to ward off harm and finally on
that vile cot he could nearly feel her, her leg seeking him out
from her own nether bed.

My wife, he thought. Then to test the sound of it he said it
aloud, but because he didn't want to share it with the animals
nearby in their cubicles he said it softly. "My wife, Francie." He
swung his legs and sat on the cot's edge, smiling, and he spoke
to her then softly. "I marry you now. Before whatever god you'd
pick, it don't matter. You're my wife and I'm your husband."

And when they talked of her from then on he called her his
wife and it was not lost on Millimaki and when he asked about
where she was or where he thought she might be Gload smiled
wistfully and Millimaki felt a terrible fear for her because he had
seen that smile before and he knew what it meant to be so spoken of by John Gload. He'd smiled telling him about a Chinaman
and about an old woman and her Pom dog sixty years dead.

Hours later while sitting in the Blazer in the shade a towering
prairie cottonwood in full leaf cast onto the shoulder of the two-
lane highway, not far from where his wife those few years ago
had come sparkling resplendent and naked from the creek, Valentine Millimaki thought perhaps he did see John Gload's point.
The cabin was still some miles south on the road. Too inhabited
yet by Glenda, he avoided it. The jail, where once he found sol-
ace in its disconnectedness from the world, seemed now to be a
stone bearing down on his neck. He stared unseeing out the
streaked windshield. Grasshoppers sizzled in the brittle weeds
and a chorus of meadowlark and red-winged blackbird filled
the cab. It was comfortable here. If not for Tom he would have
lived in the truck along the road and taken his meals there—cans

of soup eaten cold, cheese cut from the block with his pocketknife and eaten on crackers, shaving in the dimming twilight
before work beneath the dome light and sleeping across the seats
through the warming brilliant days wrapped in his jacket like a
bum and waking to the sound of passing traffic. He lurched
red-eyed through his days in a purgatory described by home and
the jail, content in neither place. A bird laboring in a hurricane
wind, moving nowhere yet unable to alight. How different
from the animated skeletons of Gload's old folks' home was he?

Among the papers on the dashboard that rose and fell with
the breeze through the side window was the letter from his
sister. He took it up and pulled it from the envelope and reread
it and then refolded the pages carefully along their creases and
put them back. On the dash it pulsed and fluttered against the
window glass. As if the words within would escape to circle his
head like carrion birds.

He'd been twelve years old. Should he have known his
mother was living life out? For his paltry sins he'd had the kind
alcoholic priest in his confessional to unburden himself to but
the transgressions against his mother seemed too great to fit in
that dim cubicle. He listed them instead in a notebook afterward,
writing them out with a gnawed pencil in a mimicry of her elegant cursive: "Disrespect." "Sullenness" (she had called it). "Slam-
ming the back door." "Didn't make my bed." Once he'd been
caught stealing a fruit pie at the little market near the school and
the proprietor had phoned. His mother related the conversation
at the dinner table in a voice so flat and shamed that it burned
his skin worse than the welts his father had later raised with the
doubled belt. He had taken him by the arm wordlessly to the
chicken shed so his sister couldn't hear the thwack of the leather
across his back, or the cries. The entries in his ledger of sins

became less frequent. "I pretended to be asleep so she would not kiss me goodnight." After six months, one or two others. He remembered the last: "The fucking slippers I knew she wouldn't ever wear." Two days later he had taken up the pencil and blacked out "fucking." That was the last time he'd opened the notebook.

The year he left for college, in the last month he'd ever stay on the ranch, he'd gone systematically from window to window to view her life and saw it reduced to four rectangles framing, whatever direction, intransigent weeds, thirsty fields lashed by wind. A barely discernible camber of earth under a sky that had yielded little but heartbreak. Scant barley, scant wheat. Pastures where their Angus browsed on knapweed and thistle. They were scabrous as dogs with mange, their ribs countable under the balding hides. The view—her life—did not change and, she knew, would not change. Even the greening of spring was to her nothing but false promise, brief April rains meted out by a prankster God for a smile. Millimaki realized then that her husband and children were no anodyne for the enormity of her despair. They had more than likely contributed to it—three more stones mortared into the wall of her private and inscrutable prison.

Without the analgesia that might have been offered by John Gload's irresistible hands, she had made one for herself with a lariat rope and a six-foot ladder.

For Glenda that same malevolent world of the outside had raised the latch and pushed open the door and had swarmed around her. Owls, snakes, coyotes. Insects leaked like sand through the door cracks to infest her hair. The wind came down from the trees to inhabit her. Did he want someday to find her, too, dangling from a collar tie or swimming in a tepid bath with her wrists blossoming gouts of red? He thought, once again, that somehow he'd become another stone in another wall.

Sweat plastered his shirt to the seatback. He looked at his watch, consulted the sun nearing its zenith to assure himself it had not spun wildly ahead in some cruel rift of time. The dog would be waiting in his kennel. He sat for a moment longer. The grass in the borrow ditch lay flat to the ground under the wind and rose again and fell and the colossal cottonwood yawed and groaned, sending down onto the truck's hood a clutch of tiny branches that clattered and skittered on the metal like juju bones.

As he rose finally to leave Gload that morning, taking his chair from the bars to the hallway, the old man had said, "Now you're the best part of my day, Valentine. I'm the same as those pitiful old sonsofbitches looking out the window at a man going to get the paper. That was a terrible thing to see and now it's me."

Gload sat watching him. Wexler leaned against the bars. The lights shone on his polished belt, his spit-shined Wellingtons. When Gload stood from his bunk Wexler pushed himself away from the bars and stood back.

"Hell, I don't bite, Weldon."

"Never said you did."

"Val, he sits right up here close."

"That's against policy. I could have him wrote up for that."

"I wish you wouldn't do that," Gload said. "As a personal favor. I kind of feel sorry for the kid."

"Any trouble he has he brings on himself. But I can let it go, sure."

"What sort of trouble?"

"Maybe 'trouble' ain't the right word. Laxadaisical is what

he is. Off hiking in the woods with that dog and one thing and another. Dirty boots like a farmer, wrinkled slacks. Thinks he has the old man's ear but he don't."

"I see what you mean."

"Dirty fingernails."

"He has let himself go, yes indeed."

"Anyways, that's what I want to talk to you about, John. I know you've got to like Millimaki but I want to say don't waste your time on him. It's time you don't have. He don't carry any whack around here. Seems like if you want to talk to somebody—for your own benefit—it ought to be me or one of the other ranking officers."

"Like Dobek maybe? He come in here with some pretty disturbing things to say, Weldon. Pretty gory stuff."

"He's a fucking animal, John."

"Kind of put the fear of God into me, I'll tell you that."

"A fucking caveman. Okay, forget Dobek." He took an incremental pace forward to illustrate his earnestness. "I'll be your man, John. If you can give me any information it might look good that you cooperated."

"I believe I have been cooperating, Weldon. What about the maps?"

Wexler sighed theatrically. "Maps didn't amount to shit, John. I think you know that."

"Them were good maps. I spent quite a little time on them."

"Didn't amount to nothing. Zero or less."

"I'm an old man, Weldon. My memory's not what it once was."

"You were fucking with me."

"Nosir." Gload rose and protested, approaching the bars with his hands extended in supplication and wearing an expression of wounded pride. "I wouldn't do any such thing."

Wexler took one step back.

"But I think I need to go on out there, Weldon. Got to walk the ground again myself. It wasn't exactly yesterday." He gripped the bars then and assumed a contemplative pose, his red-rimmed eyes to the ceiling. "What would really be best is if you were to get me a topo map of the place."

Wexler assumed his practiced pose. His hands atop his pistol butt and baton were very white. Gload watched his face. "You could do it with a topo?"

"I'm sure of it."

"A topo," he said. "Leave me think about it."

"Then we can go on out there and I could pretty well show you exactly where you want."

"Take you out? I don't believe I can do that," Wexler said.

"Right, right. The Old Man would probably want Val to take me out, if at all."

"I outrank Millimaki, time in grade."

"I'm just going by what I hear around here."

"Like what?"

"Like he was going to let Val take me out there in a set of leg chains, that's all." Gload chuckled, held out his hands, now in a gesture of helplessness. "As if a old sonofabitch like me could leg it out anyways."

FOURTEEN

He sat in his chair alone in the small garden reading the *Great Falls Tribune*. Francie that morning had gone to town as she had nearly every day for the past several days and after he'd read the single column about Sidney White, he laid aside the paper and sat looking at the crocuses she'd planted, unfurling their color around the base of a lilac tree. She'd planted tulip and daffodils there too and the crocus blooms stood among the deep green serpent's tongues of their emerging leaves like drops of paint. White had been arrested for rape and a separate charge of assault and battery in Miles City, where little more than a week ago Gload had left him with his money and had driven away with an abscess of misgiving festering in his stomach. The girl had been fifteen years old and White had gotten her drunk and taken her to the room and the next day the girl's father had come and White had beaten the man with a golf club from a set he'd apparently stolen from an unlocked car parked in the hotel lot. The article stated that he had also employed that implement in his assault on the girl, details withheld. He was awaiting trial in the Custer County jail.

Gload took up the paper once again and reread the article slowly and carefully and sat back against the chair shaking his head wearily. "Golf clubs," he said.

The countryside was still as a painting, the wind strangely becalmed and even the sky to the south where he gazed was without moving clouds and against the azure backdrop was not a starling, not a gull. Gload, undistracted before the motionlessness of his beloved view, in a very short time made his decision and as was his way, from that moment, he did not reconsider it or waver from its necessary course. He pushed himself up from his chair and laid aside the folded paper on the small table beside his cup and shambled through the dewy grass in his odd sailor's gait to the tool bin behind the house. When he returned with the proper implements thrown over his shoulder he paused briefly at the lilac and stood looking down at Francie's flowers and then continued on, past the chair and down the lane among the trees.

The evening before, he sat in the same chair at the same table. The dinner he had made for them warmed in the oven. A maelstrom of dust billowing redly in the sunset heralded her arrival and shortly the car pulled down the lane and stopped near the house. She came up the drive, slightly drunk and walking with great care as if negotiating a patch of ice. She smiled blearily at him. When she sat he could smell the smoke of the bar on her and she seemed to have applied more makeup since she'd left in the morning, more musky scent.

"Home is the hunter, home from the hills," she recited. "Home is the hunter, stoned to the gills."

"If you're talking about me, I'm not the one stoned to the gills," John Gload said. "At no six o'clock in the afternoon."

"Oh, Johnny. Be nice. I just had a nice afternoon."

"Doing what?"

"Visiting. A nice afternoon of visiting."

"Visiting in the bar, that would be."

"Yes. That would be."

"It just isn't dignified a woman your age in a bar."

"Oh, God," she said. "Dignity." She sat heavily, her legs thrust out. Her heels furrowed the dirt and in the rumpled hose the flesh of her legs seemed to sag from their bones.

"Why can't you just stay here? You got everything you need."

From the chair she gazed out vacantly, reached out without looking and patted the huge hand on the tabletop opposite her. "I care for you, Johnny, I do. But not everything. Not hardly."

"What do you need I haven't brought here for you? You tell me what it is and I'll try and get it."

"It's not things. I don't need things. You know that never meant nothing to me."

"What, then?"

"People, Johnny. The company of people. I'm not like you. You who could sit here alone in that chair for a week."

"I was people last time I checked."

"But you're your own world and I always have known that. You don't really need me and it's okay. I understand that and it's okay, it really is. I know you care about me, but I just need to see myself in other people."

"I do need you. I wisht you wouldn't say shit like that."

"Okay, you do."

"You say see yourself in other people. Good Christ, Francie. Let me tell you. People aren't mirrors. If they were, what you seen looking back at you would make your hair stand up. You don't want to see that."

Her hair had fallen in her eyes and she swept it back. Lipstick she had applied with a trembling hand earlier was blurred at the corner of her mouth.

"Just real people," she repeated.

"Bar people. Christ. They're not real people."

"They're real enough, John. And not all of them are drunks. Some people just go there for the socializing. Just to sit and gab."

"And to drink."

"A little bit of wine. Just because it's not something you do, because it's not Johnny's vice, doesn't make it bad necessarily. It makes me feel good. How can you not want that for me?"

"And who are they? A bunch of hayseeds and half-assed ranch hands. Dipshit farmers with their fat hands all over you."

"You used to be one. You told me so. You were a farmer yourself."

"I was a goddamn kid."

"And I don't need to be touched, Johnny. That's not it at all." She looked at him then and reached to stroke his dure cheek. John Gload stared at the ground.

"Yeah, well I'll tell you what *they* see. See a set of breasts and a vagina."

She laughed out loud. "Oh, God, you kill me, John. Vagina. In your way you are such a prude."

Looking long out over the trees and the sage flats, amber as an August wheat field beneath the dust of her earlier passing, she began to hum, a near imperceptible evocation of wind or of an infant mewing in a distant room. Gload leaned his ear toward her across the weather-checked tabletop to discern what air it was that had so quickly taken her and in so doing beheld for the first time the minute nodding affirmations of a palsy. He was reminded suddenly of a nun who'd been kind to him at the orphanage and the name they had given her affliction, St. Vitus' dance. Despite its name summoning images of whirling happiness, it was nonetheless for Gload ever after a sign of pitiful age. She had had a man's name, Bernard he thought, and she'd died one day nodding at her desk in front of a classroom of children, all horrified but one.

She hummed. Her eyes slowly closed as though by her own lullaby she slipped softly into sleep.

"What if I wasn't here?" he said.

She said dreamily, "Oh, let's not talk about that. You'll always be here to be my anchor."

"Dragging you down you mean."

"No, John. Holding me in place."

She turned in her chair and took his hand in both of hers atop the table. "We're okay now because I'm home to you and we'll have a nice dinner and we can sit and watch the sun go down if you want like two beautiful people in a movie. Can we do that, Johnny? I don't want to fight with you."

"Yeah. We can do that."

"Don't be mad at me. I can't take that."

"All right. I ain't mad at you."

"Did you make something? I smell something good."

"Just a roast. Nothing special."

"No, it sounds wonderful."

"And carrots and baby potatoes with the skin left on."

That night at her dressing table the woman John Gload would later call his wife sat massaging lotion onto her hands with a wringing motion and then with the backs of her hands patting the soft loose folds beneath her chin. All the while she stared at the image in the mirrors. From the bed Gload, feigning sleep, watched her. She tugged back the graying hair at her temples to dissolve for a moment the creases that swarmed about her eyes. Her hair was still thick as a horse's mane and Gload loved to lock his thick fingers in it. She touched at the corners of her lips, the cleft beneath her nose and then as if her arms could no longer support their weight, her hands collapsed to rest among the jars and tubes of ointments and balms, and the trembling that had recently befallen her set the tiny fluted vials of her perfumes with their jewel-like glass stoppers chittering softly. From the vanity's three mirrors three images stared out, each with red eyes brimming with the recognition of slow and irre versible decline.

After a time Gload hazarded a look and found her still sitting, and he watched with one burning eye the three images there until she rose from her stool stately and a little unsteady and came one last time to share their bed.

When he was done he stood back and it was a quaint agrarian pose he struck, the man stropping his face and neck with a bandana and leaning on the spud bar and behind him the slender black boles of the apple trees etched against a sky of splendrous color. He'd dug many such holes but none so fine or so deep. The sod and thin rich topsoil were laid aside in one pile, the stones and gravel he struggled through in another, and with a square-nosed shovel he'd skived the hole's edges sharp and plumb as though it might be entered in a county fair. It had taken him most of the day and at noon he'd walked back to the house to eat a pear and drink two glasses of water and then had returned to his work, clambering down into the hole with the leaned metal spud bar for support. He encountered rocks the size of men's heads as he went down and the roots of the apple trees like cables as the hole took its shape and he was forced to chop them away with the short-handled ax he'd brought. In doing so he feared for the life of the trees but he had little choice and hoped finally that the roots would take hold anew when the hole was filled.

He stopped frequently in the course of his endeavors, leaning on the polished shovel handle or on the long metal bar with its spaded end and shaking his head in amused resignation at the ravages of his advancing age. Still, he heaved obdurate stones from the hole that would have given trouble to much younger men and he drew satisfaction from that.

The sun he had welcomed early for its warmth on his face and that had scalded his neck later now threw his long shadow across the hole. He saw a large red stone in a corner of the hole that might cause discomfort to whoever rested there, so he clambered back down and with the long-handled bar prized the intransigent stone from its place where it had lain for ten thousand years and threw it out. Once again at the hole's edge he assessed it and checked its depth against the length of the bar and declared himself satisfied.

Had she been looking closely she might have seen the piles of fresh soil among the orchard trees but she wasn't. She had tilted down the car's rearview mirror as she drove down the lane and seemed to be studying herself in it. John Gload was once again in his chair. He had showered and changed out of his soaked and foul coveralls and shirt and his wet hair was plastered along his head. She swung open the door and stepped out and stood unsteadily before him.

"Now what'd you go and do?" he said.

"I thought it might make your old hag look a little younger."

"It's red."

"Auburn, Johnny." She pulled a strand of hair in front of her face and looked at it. "You don't like it," she said.

"I do like it. I like it quite a little bit." The chair creaked as he stood up and he took her by the hand. Like a child she allowed herself to be led inside, as she walked woodenly still examining a strand of hair. He said, "You look like a million bucks."

There was a small short lamp on the table in the modest dining room and in its pool of wan light they ate their dinner wordlessly. Her juice glass held her favorite sweet wine, the color of gasoline. She watched John Gload eat, the fork in his fist like a fork from a child's tea set. But he was neat and his manners were oddly courtly and she smiled at him over the rim of her glass. Afterward they sat in the chairs at the little table outside the door that Gload favored to read his newspaper. The river rolling in its primordial channel was invisible but clouds lay above it, a pale serpentine parody, kinetic and aswim with gulls. They spoke little and Francie seemed happy to listen to the conversations of small birds from the arbor, and from their cool holes the shrill piping of ground squirrels. The tops of the hills behind the house were softly aflame with scarlet sunset and they watched mule deer walk unalarmed through the conflagration like the prophets of Daniel.

She had refilled her glass after dinner and brought it with her, in her unstable state bearing it before her two-handed like a ciborium. When she drank the last of it and set the glass down her hand trembled. "Oh, my," she said. Gload had been watching and laid his hand over hers as though warming a young bird fallen from its nest.

"Why don't you go lay down for a while," he said. "I'll take care of that little bit of dishes."

"You wouldn't mind?"

"Go on. You look wore out."

"You're not supposed to say that to a lady."

He looked into her eyes and they were laced with red, her face with its faded makeup was ashen and the lines beneath her eyes and at the corners of her mouth seemed drawn with ink. "You look tired is all. How's that?"

"Oh, it doesn't matter."

He stood at the sink when he'd finished, watching a spring storm form up in the east, newly arrived birds roiling up before the verdigris clouds like autumn leaves. The water ran from the tap and after a long while he noticed it and screwed down the handles and stood once again looking out.

He came from the closet holding it, saying to her in a whisper, "I always liked this on you." The thin beige draperies rose and riffled on the breeze and the sky framed in the window sash was streaked with distant rain. The room had taken on an odd green cast. He sat in a chair by the bed for some time, watching her sleep and he held across his arms like an offering the green dress he had bought for her one year on a trip to Billings. Storm clouds drug their tentacles across the sageland ten miles to the east but he could smell the rain on the air. As if it grew in a window box he could smell the sage. Then he stood, still watching her, with the bed's other pillow in his hands.

Her movements under him he thought were not unlike those of their lovemaking, her squirming and bucking and even when she stopped and he pulled the pillow away her face was dreamy, her eyes half-closed as if on the verge of mere gratified sleep or rapture.

Gload removed her clothes and laid them aside—they smelled

of the bar, perhaps of other men—and he buttoned on the green dress that had been his favorite, his huge brutal hands fumbling at the buttons and impossible hooks and at an antique collar pin she had treasured. "This makes your eyes look greener," he said, but he spoke of an image of memory only, as in fact the light was gone from them and what he could see beneath the half-closed papery lids seemed leached of color.

From the bureau he selected one of her handkerchiefs, its edges trimmed in lace. He held it to his nose, folded it neatly, and put it in a rear pocket. He slid his hands beneath her, at neck and knees, and took her up. She weighed nothing. At the hole he bent and laid her in the grass gently as if to prevent waking her and went around to the opposite side and slid down into the cool of the earth. He lifted her once again and laid her down, arranging the folds of the dress around her legs modestly, and he crossed her arms on her chest, thought better of it and laid them beside her in the hole. Raindrops now, like falling coins, rattled through the sage south of the orchard. He touched her cheek, her hair newly red, laid the handkerchief over her face and climbed with difficulty out of the hole for the third time. With the spade he had left there leaned against a tree for that purpose he covered her over, not looking down but working at the two piles with an easy rhythm and listening to his own breathing, to the call of birds among the trees and the rain in earnest then hissing in the branches.

That night he lay on the selfsame bed and called on his dream of plowing, furrowing the ground over and over as the landscape reeled past and kits took his scent and the gulls came. Sleep, though, would not come and so he lay smoking in the dark. He strained to hear above the wind the pong of suspended harrow tines. Rain lashed the windowpanes and muddied the grassless square plot in the apple trees and John Gload imagined a voracious reticulum of roots beneath the orchard plot stirring, then writhing like a nest of snakes and finally, in the damp dark, winning purchase once again in earth, in bones.

The day following was warm and windy and he spent it putting the house in good order. He hosed off his digging tools and hung them in the shed. He aligned her shoes at the bottom of the closet and he washed and hung her clothes. Several times he went down the lane and from various points stood looking into the grove of greening fruit trees, the weave of their wild, untended branches astir with birds. He waited each time to hear the clash of his rustic windchime and then he went slewing back up the road.

He was standing so in the lane two days later with his hands in his rear pockets when he saw the dust of the approaching patrol cars and he went again unhurriedly to his garden chair to wait. Since the brief rains the twisted copse was furred with inchoate green, at his feet the crocuses and breaching tulips, nodding trumpets of the daffodils, yellow beyond yellow in the sun.

FIFTEEN

In later years, and at unexpected times, the thought came to him that it had been a ridiculous place for his life to come apart and it took little more than a linoleum pattern beneath his feet or the jangle of dropped silverware to dizzy him and make his mouth go dry.

He'd gone to the hospital shortly before noontime. In the ICU waiting room he sat across from an elderly woman who held in one sclerous hand a rosary of bloodred beads, covering her eyes with the other as though unable to bear the sight of the world beyond her memories. He'd fallen asleep in the plastic chair with his head lolling and his mouth ajar and he had nearly missed her as she swept through with one arm stuck in the sleeve of an overcoat as though she were going out somewhere. He'd not seen her in two weeks and his heart throbbed at the sight of her. She had grown thinner and her hair was cut in some new way. He asked her to lunch and she stood frozen looking at him with her arm in the coat and then looking for a long moment beyond him and she seemed to be making some kind of decision. She said she did not have much time but that they could eat in the cafeteria. They rode the elevator in silence, Val staring foolishly at her white shoes, at her perfect calves in their nurse's hose, white as bandages.

He had taken a tray and absently pointed at a stack of grilled cheese sandwiches. She would not eat anything and she chose a table in the center of the crowded cafeteria.

He set the tray down and when they sat he said, "How are things going?"

"They're going fine."

He pointed to the coat she had draped over the corner of the table. "Were you going out somewhere for lunch?"

"Not really."

"Not really? You were or you weren't."

"You don't need to talk to me like that, Val. I'm not one of your perps."

"That's not a word anybody says. That's a TV word."

"Well, Val, my point is I'm not an investigation."

"No, it's just that you were going somewhere because you had your coat so you were going out. I don't have to be a cop to figure that."

Her hands were in her lap hidden from him by the table and she stared into them.

"I am so tired of it, Val."

He looked at her. "If you could tell me what 'it' is, I would appreciate it."

"It," she said. At the serving line a metal tray was dropped and it clattered on the floor, the silverware skittering. "Struggling. Tired of struggling."

He studied her across the table. Her hair was a kind of short boy cut and there were streaks of lighter blond in it. In the hollow of her lovely slender neck rested a tiny silver dolphin on a strand of chain, a charm he had not given her and had never seen before and at the sight of it the blood drained from everywhere and seemed to pool cold in the bottom of his stomach. Her words after that fell on his head like blows, forcing his eyes to the floor where he beheld the linoleum's pattern swimming and blurred.

"We seem to struggle at everything," she said. "To find the energy to talk. To find time to be who we really are."

"Riddles. These are just crazy riddles, goddamn it, Glenda." He swung his eyes up to her face briefly. "I know who I am. But I look at you now and I think maybe you're finding out you're somebody else. That you're making yourself into somebody else."

"That's just it exactly, Val. You've always known who you were. But I was just a part of you. And I'm seeing that being part of you isn't enough. It's not fair to me."

He was close to weeping in frustration. "I never said anything ever, did I? Jesus. Fair? It wasn't like I ever said don't change anything. I wouldn't have cared about your hair."

"Christ, Val, it isn't about my hair."

With his head bowed he looked to be a man at prayer. His clasped hands as he sought to maintain some grasp on the world were white and the veins in his forearms stood out. But the world became in an instant nothing more than a sphere encompassing the two of them, a metal tray, a tabletop—all else beyond an indiscernible realm without meaning.

"No, not your hair," he said. "Not about your hair at all but about somebody else, about some other motherfucker." He stopped and breathed deeply. He stared at the floor. "It's a doc-tor, am I correct? And maybe he's the bwana with all the dead heads in his house and the fucking tasseled shoes. Is he here right now? I'll bet the fucker's here right now." He made a show of looking around the room, though he could have seen noth-ing at that moment beyond the end of his arm. "It's like a bad movie, like a movie you've seen a hundred times."

"I didn't say it was anyone." Her voice came at him flat and cold.

"But it is."

There seemed not the slightest bit of shame in her. She looked straight ahead at nothing. She took a breath. "I have been seeing someone."

He forced himself to raise his head and he wore a look of incredulity. "You're married to *me*. You can't be *seeing* someone."

"Nevertheless."

The security guard rose with some effort from behind a table where he'd been reading a newspaper. His shirt hung from his distended paunch and as he walked toward them he tucked the tails into the tops of his trousers. He stood beside the table with his hands crossed and resting atop his stomach. Indistinct tat-toos on the back of one wrist and above each knuckle. He stood for some time looking from Millimaki to his wife and listening. Finally Millimaki looked up. The man was in his sixties and wore a utility belt hung with keys and a flashlight and a canister of mace.

"We're having a private conversation."

"Not all that private, Deputy, it turns out, because I could hear it over yonder."

"This is private."

"Maybe this ain't the place for this sort of business."

Millimaki ignored him. Glenda said, "We're just leaving."

"We're not just leaving."

"Deputy," the man said. "Conductation of this business to be done elsewhere."

Through the sudden diminishment of the world the man had become a vague and watery shape uttering words from far away. Millimaki glanced briefly to his left. "Fuck off. That's not even a word."

"Val, stop it."

"Fuck your conductation." He brought his hands up to the tabletop, his fists clenched. His ears rang strangely, as if he'd been clubbed.

"And it's a doctor," he said. "Couldn't it have been at least a fucking janitor?"

"It doesn't matter who it is."

"And he gave you that chain, is that not correct? That fish." He'd meant to point but as if they did not belong to him his hands rose toward her pale neck in a clutching gesture.

Her hand went reflexively to her throat. "Please please stop."

"A fucking doctor," he repeated. "All this mystery about doctors, all this, whatever, glorification." His voice was rising. People at the nearby tables had begun to stare. "All the fucking mystery. Cutting and sawing and rooting around. Christ, they're high-priced carpenters. They're nothing."

The guard said, "Deputy, I'm asking please."

Glenda buried her face in her hands, not crying, not ashamed, Val noted, but merely embarrassed.

Through her fingers she said wearily, "Oh, Val."

"I would cut every goddamn one of them from crotch to eyeball, I swear to Christ."

She took down her hands. Her perfect face was hard and

smooth as topaz. In a harsh whisper she said, "My God, Val. You're scaring people. You're wearing a gun. That scares people."

He leaned closer to her, the silver neck charm inches from his face. "Okay," he whispered. "Exactly. And how about if I take this gun and shove it up your doctor's ass? I could do that. I could do that just for a smile."

"That's enough, Val. This is a public place."

The security guard had been staring at Glenda's throat or perhaps trying to see down the front of her uniform. His left hand hovered near the mace canister at his belt. "Like the young lady says, pardner," he said. "Not here, not at this time."

"Yes," Millimaki said. "A public place. And it just now occurred to me why you decided to tell me all this here, because of your misguided idea that I would not do anything to embarrass you and this is the part where you're oh so very fucking wrong." He wiped a sleeve across his eyes and stood up. From the foggy periphery of his vision he noted the shape of the guard moving toward him. "Ladies and gentlemen, I am a Copper County sheriff's deputy officer can I have your attention I am a law enforcement officer and my wife has just informed me she is *seeing someone* and please remain calm. I assure all present that should he be here I will not at this time discharge my firearm into the anal region of the medical professional who is fucking my wife."

Two days later he sat lacing his boots on a long varnished bench in the locker room at the end of his shift, through the diamond mesh of the high windows a luminous light the color of wheat. He did not look up at the sound of boot heels coming down the row of lockers.

John Gload that night had been more reticent than usual and sat smoking quietly in his cell in the dark. The night wore on. Even the craziest of the men in their cages were subdued, as though the old man had cast a spell on them that he might have peace for his night's plowing and eventual sleep. Millimaki had himself barely slept since his seizure of grief and rage at the hospital and his shift beneath the tube lights had seemed without end.

Now Voyle Dobek stood over him. "I seen you in the park talking to Gload," he said. Against the bright backdrop of the morning's light, when Millimaki looked up, Dobek's figure was in shadow, his breath that close a nauseating admixture of coffee and Skoal. Millimaki's stomach lurched. The act of lacing his boots in his state of exhaustion seemed impossible work. He stared stupidly at hands suddenly as inept as a toddler's. Beside his scuffed boot toes Dobek's spit-shined Wellingtons were dazzling.

"How can you sit and talk to a piece of shit like that?" Dobek said.

"Which exactly piece of shit would we be talking about, Voyle? I thought they were all pieces of shit to you."

"Your old psycho." He effected a nasal sound of disgust. "The way you sit out there."

"You pretty much nailed it, Voyle. Two guys, a bench, the exchange of words. That's how it's done."

"No, that ain't the way you do it, asshole. Not out there."

"Out where?"

"Out in the public. Where the civilians can see you."

"Haven't noticed anybody watching."

"You'd be surprised. The fuckers see everything."

"I don't know what there is to see, Voyle. Two guys sitting on a bench."

"There's a right fucking way and a wrong fucking way is what I'm telling you and you don't sit out there with a psycho piece of shit for the citizens to see. If *you* don't give a shit." He waved a hand vaguely about the vacant room. "It looks bad on us."

"I'm very sorry, Officer Dobek," Millimaki said. "To make you look bad would just about ruin my whole entire day."

"I had you pegged as a smart-ass from the minute you come on. I was willing to give you the benefit of the doubt. But then I don't know." He straightened his back, looked around the room as if to address an audience. "Heard about your little performance up at the hospital. I guess if my wife was fucking some doctor, it might make me out to be a smart-ass too."

Because he was sitting down and had to come up off the bench as he swung, the uppercut caught Dobek squarely in the groin and Millimaki felt the soft give of the man's balls. His fist seemed to disappear and he had just enough time to pull back before the big man fell, clattering to the floor like a bagful of loose change as his billy, keys, cuffs and gun butt hit the tile. When from the other side of the lockers men came running, Val was astride the man's back with his nightstick under Dobek's chin and may well have choked him to death as he remembered nothing. He had heard the word "wife" come from Dobek's mouth, later remembered just that, as if like a cartoon voice balloon it hung in the air, or like a plume of winter breath, and after that there was nothing—a void washed in red.

As if drunk he arrived home with no memory either of the drive and he sat in his recliner staring out at the scarcely moving portraiture of the brilliant day—clouds, quavering branches heavy with leaf, a nervous sparrow on the windowsill. He became aware of a terrible odor and got up and walked about

the room and sniffed at the dog, asleep on his bed. "You didn't
puke somewhere, Tom, did you, bud?" He walked into the empty
bedroom and found the smell there too and realized it was him,
on him. He shucked his pants and saw the stain on his knees
then, vomit he must have knelt in while riding Voyle Dobek
like some giant tortoise in a crimson sea of oblivion.

Even as Millimaki closed the office door, the sheriff said, "I
don't know what it is but we've got to get at this problem and
solve it right fucking now."

"Yes, sir."

"My ass, 'Yes, sir.' Spit it out, Val. I cannot have my officers
killing each other in the locker room."

"It was a difference of opinion."

"Yes, no shit." He called, "Raylene." Shortly the secretary's
head appeared in the door. "Raylene, would you please do me
the favor of going down to the dispensary and getting me some
aspirin."

"There's some right there in front of you, in the drawer."

"I've been looking for it for fifteen minutes."

"Oh, all right. For goodness' sake, if your head wasn't
attached."

He listened to her heels clack-clacking down the marble
hallway.

"She is a wonderful woman but cursed with a lively curiosity and a certain lack of discretion in matters concerning
interdepartmental conflict. If you understand. I don't have a
headache, not counting, metaphorically, you and Dobek."

"I understand."

"And did you in fact blindside Officer Dobek in the locker room as he came around the corner?"

Millimaki stared at him.

"I didn't think so. And I might add that it speaks well for you that no one has come forward to corroborate his dim recollection of events."

"There wasn't anybody around at the time."

"That doesn't sometimes make a bit of difference."

"It was just me and him there."

"I imagine before the day is out Raylene will be able to tell me exactly what happened, but if you'd like to speed the process."

"It was a difference—"

"Of fucking opinion. Yes, I got that the first time."

"He said something about my wife."

The sheriff stood up then, raked a hand through his newly barbered hair, and called out, "Raylene." There was no answer. He said, "You know that I know what kind of a cop Dobek is, Val, do you not? What kind of man?"

"I have no way of knowing."

"Well, goddamn it, yes you do. You see these two round things on the front of my face?"

"Yes, sir."

"Voyle is just a guy who's been around too long and somewhere or other took the other course." He examined his nails. "He is a burdensome man."

Millimaki said, "It's not what started it but he seemed to object to me talking to Gload."

"Did you tell him I asked you to?"

"No, sir. I guess I figured that was between you and me."

"I'll talk to Voyle about that. In the meantime you're taking two days off. My suggestion, from the look of you, would be to try and sleep most of that time." He stood with his hands on the desktop, his pale eyes looking beyond Val's head to the door, and called out once again to his secretary. When he got no response he said, "Your behavior is not acceptable, Deputy Millimaki, and will not be tolerated. That being said, I would have done the same thing to that big prick and if a word of that last sentence leaves this room other than in your thick head you will be gone forever and I would not recommend you for a crossing guard." Into the ensuing quiet came the rapid clacking of Raylene's heels down the corridor and the sheriff said, "And now I'm going to on account of you have to take two aspirins I don't need because she'll sure as hell sit here and watch me. So I have you to blame also for the subsequent heartburn." He sat abruptly into his chair. "You'll not be seen here until your shift Thursday night." By way of augmenting his performance, as Raylene came into the room he said gruffly, "First and last warning, Deputy Millimaki. Now get your ass out of here."

That night he sat at his table once again and the fire of old lodgepole he had set in the fireplace veered and swayed with the wind that came down the old river rock chimney. The flames rose up suddenly, flaring high into the pipe as though like a sprite or comet they would escape out into the night and leave a cold jumble of blackened logs on the grate. The dog raised his head from his extended paws and stared at the fire. He looked at Millimaki and with a sigh lay back again with his square snout atop his forelegs and the fire moaned up the flue. In the brief silences lulls in the wind afforded Millimaki could hear coyotes in the hills calling across the dark.

He slept on the couch opposite the fire, wrapped in a quilt

his sister had given them for a wedding present and through his sleep low shapes prowled, only their slavering mouths visible, phosphorescent as seafoam, snuffling at the cupboard doors and running their rough tongues along the cutting board where he'd earlier trimmed a piece of meat, and in the dream the shapeless predators clawing at the walls and floorboards as if seeking something and not finding it turned their glowing muzzles toward him.

When he awoke the front door stood rocking open on its antique hinges, the trapezoid of milky light it admitted falling across the kitchen floor and illuminating a shirring flotsam of brittle box elder leaves. With his heart throbbing wildly against the planks of his ribs he latched the door and shot home the old-fashioned slidebolt and in his bare feet went about the house holding a pair of fire tongs like a baseball bat, throwing light switches and moving into the three small side rooms, looking behind doors and inside closets. He suddenly felt foolish, standing in his own bedroom with sooty hands around the tongs. His pistol hung in its belt from a chairback in the kitchen. "Tongs," he said aloud. "You're a dangerous man." He went to the outer room and added a split of pine to the coals, stirring them alive with the fire tongs, and curled once more in the goose down as the breathing embers provoked the dog's smoldering eyes from the dark.

Hours later his eyes opened to window light golden as grain dust and Tom sat staring into his face as though willing him awake for his breakfast.

SIXTEEN

The elms in full leaf shuddered above him and through the verdure he could make out an occasional star, a shard of moon. From their secret fissures in the courthouse dome, bats came afield, darting even beneath the trees for the legions of big moths so abundant there that night they blundered against Millimaki's face like the brush of an eyelash.

For his lunch he had an apple and a hard roll he had found in the bread drawer at home, having no idea of its age other than it was somewhere short of old enough to grow mold. He had a four-inch round of hard salami and on the bench under the elms he alternated bites of meat and bread and for dessert ate the apple, cold and hard, while stretched out on the bench like a vagrant, one hand behind his head and his eyes on the stars that sought him out beneath the green cupola.

When he used the bathroom on his return to the jail, the haggard face in the mirror above the sink wore on its forehead a smudge of moth soot like the ashes left from a priest's thumb long years ago.

When Millimaki returned to escort duty after his involuntary time off, the old killer had grown more fond and familiar, taking the deputy's hand in his between the bars and holding it there a long while. He seemed troubled by Millimaki's silences and stared at him with basset hound eyes. Wexler in Millimaki's absence had been Gload's escort and companion but the old man spoke little of him. "My pal Weldon," he would say. "My old buddy Weldon." Despite frequent inquiries Millimaki divulged little more than that his wife at the end of her day stayed with a girl-friend in town. It might be true, he thought. It might be true.

Gload, an inveterate reader of newspapers, had noted that county extension agents statewide were predicting record har-vests and absurd per-bushel prices. Millimaki sat with a letter from his sister in his lap and Gload spoke of machinery and the cost of diesel fuel, in the slant of surgical light from the over-head fluorescents figuring and refiguring on his yellow legal pad the amount of money he and his father might have realized from harvesting the field of his dreams, imagining that sere and rocky plot an animated gilded drapery of ripe wheat. He seemed very much taken with the notion.

"Can that be right," he said incredulously, "five dollars a bushel?"

Millimaki glanced up briefly. "I guess it is, if that's what the paper says."

"You're in the wrong business, Valentine. You ought to of stayed on the farm. You'd have chains on your neck and a Coupe de Ville under your ass."

"I don't think it would look too good on me," Millimaki said distantly.

Gload returned to his calculations, his huge disembodied hands like cumbersome string puppets moving across the yellow page. It was near three in the morning and Millimaki sat with his legs crossed reading his sister's letter and eating a sandwich made of cheese and bread which he balanced on his knee. News of her daughter, her husband, news of a world that seemed of another universe. The world for these men was reduced to floor, ceiling, walls, and bars, and his own differed little—an unfixed cubicle of solitude that, like a carapace, went with him everywhere and was impervious to the warming sun or the wind in the trees or even the unconditional affections of a sister who seemed not to care he did not write in return and send his love, which she deserved.

He ate. The dry bread and questionable cheese turned to a clot of clay in his mouth. He read the letter to the end and considered the PS which again conveyed his sister's desire to solve the mystery of their mother. Of their abandonment. "PS," she wrote. "Do you think Daddy had someone else?" But no. He'd barely had enough affection for the three of them and Millimaki could not imagine the old man mustering the energy to lavish embraces and scalding forbidden kisses on some other, the flame he carried in his tight paunch barely sufficient to propel him through the days and seasons and years of numbing labor. Little but stone remained of him at the end of the day. The extent of his tenderness in all the years was an occasional squeeze of the shoulder or a tousle of the hair. He had seen his parents kiss only once.

From the shadowed recess of John Gload's cell the old man's voice came softly: "I have got one letter in my whole life," nearly a whisper, as if the presence of a man there reading a letter merely stirred a memory which he may have shared with the darkness, may not even have spoken aloud. "It was from the maid in the house where I spent some years as a kid. I can remember the whole thing, but only because it was short. The nigger gal's name was Vera Blue. She said, 'Dear John-Jee, Miss Goldie dead from a stomach sickness down here in Thermopolis. She asked about you at the end. I thought you would want to know she was dead. From a stomach cancer. Your friend, Vera Blue.' That's it, word for word." Gload made his chuckling noise. "Ain't that a kick? If I could get rid of old worthless shit like that out of my head I'd have room for more important stuff."

Millimaki said, "I'm sorry. What?" He stared blankly at the writing on the page and the old man's voice, so soft and distant, had barely registered. He'd only half heard. "What stuff?"

"Hell, kid, I don't know. Algebra maybe, or the business with triangles and shapes and all. That always interested me. What's that, geometry?"

"I believe it is."

"Those old Greeks or whatever they were and their geometry. Or Romans. And how about this while we're at it. Been stuck in my head for, hell, fifty, sixty years. I read it of all places off the back of a little fancy pillow: *Ex nihilo nihil fit*. Probably didn't say it right but I goddamn remember how it was spelled." Which he did, letter by letter for Millimaki's benefit, in the end rapping the smooth dome of his skull with his knuckles. "Now how did that stay in there? Don't even know what lingo that is."

"It's Latin," Millimaki said, "but I don't know what it means exactly."

"By God, you are a college boy."

"More because I was an altar boy."

"Sweet Jesus, an altar boy." Gload made the blowing noise that replicated a laugh. "I'm partnered up with a goddamn altar boy."

Val sat back, folded the letter carefully and returned it to its envelope. He sat tapping it on the heel of his boot. He picked up the sandwich and looked at what remained for a moment and threw it into the paper bag. From the tenebrous cages issued the snores and rustlings of his charges which in the previous long months had become as familiar to him as wind in the box elders around his home. After several minutes, from the near darkness, he heard John Gload say, "I can take it, Valentine. Nobody needs to be out there defending my honor."

Millimaki stared into the ink of the old man's cell. He could, as before, only see Gload's hands, now folded like a schoolboy's atop his writing desk.

"You've lost me," he said.

"I've dealt with cops would make him look like a goddamn fairy princess. He ain't nothing."

Millimaki thought the old man may have slipped off into his secret netherworld yet again, as he had after Sidney White had been brought in, so he merely sat and said nothing.

"You hear me, Val? Dobek's nothing but shit in a shirt. Don't be getting yourself strung out on account of me."

"What the hell are you talking about?"

"Heard about your little dust-up. And I do appreciate it, don't get me wrong."

"Somebody around here ought to have his lips riveted. And whatever you think, you think wrong. That had not one goddamn thing to do with you."

"All right, Deptee."

"Nothing to do with you and furthermore none of your goddamn business, either."

In his cage Gload was smiling, his brutal illuminated hands piously folded. "Yessir," he said.

Millimaki's sleeplessness worsened. No combination of the sheriff's beer elixir or Moon's organic pills provided relief. He shifted fitfully on the recliner or the couch beneath strangling sheets. He tried sleeping on an air mattress set in front of the fireplace and he tried the same arrangement on the open porch and was beset by mosquitoes. The one place he would not sleep or attempt to sleep was the bed he had shared with Glenda, where the most invidious ghost of all those that populated his hours, awake and asleep, resided.

In a snatch of sleep in his porch chair he dreamt his wife approaching in a strange bridal bedizenment of soiled bandages, a rope of intravenous tubes accoutering her neck. She walked up the lane in her gown of rags but seemed to come no nearer as though her small feet could find no purchase but her smile was as luminous as the sun. And so by the time he made his way from the porch chair to the jangling phone his heart hammered in his chest. It was not undone. Such portent in dream was not the stuff of mere wishing because what power do we have to shape our dreams? He could reason. He could even plead. Millimaki's hand above the phone trembled.

But it was not his wife and perhaps it was not her either in the dream but some other luminous creature meant to torment him with her apocryphal smile. He'd been home for less than three hours and had slept little of that time and so when he set

out to search for the girl unaccountably lost among the blank
tableland grain fields of Pondera County he was in sorry
plight—burning eyes, the taste of ashes in his mouth. His heart
chugged in his chest dull and distant and his veins seemed to
pump lead to his sodden limbs. But awake, at least, he was not
at the mercy of his dreams, a wilderness of guile where he wandered lost and powerless.

"You don't have to go," the sheriff said. "I could call over to
Silver Bow and have them send someone."

Val looked down at his feet in the worn leather moccasins.
He looked out the window at the cottonwoods far down along
the creek, and the water glimpsed among the trunks and quavering leaves ran sleek and aluminum like the backs of the cut-
throat in their secret holes. Another day, what seemed long ago,
he and his wife might have gone there together.

"That's all right, Sheriff. Tom could use the work."

"You sure about this? I know you haven't had time for much
sleep."

The skewed apparitional Glenda still lingered in his head.
"Sleep," he said wistfully. "No, sir. I just figured out here recently
it's overrated. I just need to get dressed and load my gear."

Wexler let himself in through the sally gate and went along the
corridor with a martial air, looking neither left nor right and
ignoring the sounds from behind the bars that followed him.
His name sung in falsetto. Kissing noises. Moans of mock
ecstasy. There would be time enough, he thought. And Dobek
since his humiliation in the locker room would require little
urging to exercise his rage on these animals in the blind hours
of the night. In and out, a visitation as silent as a priest. At that

hour bruises and broken teeth became mere figments sprung
from the delirium of caged men. They may slip and fall. And
who knew but that they might inflict such pain upon themselves?

Thus comforted he stood before John Gload's cell door.
The old man looked up. The pencil he held was little more than
three inches long, worn from his fevered doodling and geo-
ponic tabulations and he held it up.

"I could use a new pencil, Weldon."

"I'll see about it."

"And where's our friend Deputy Millimaki?"

Wexler snorted. "Off with Rin Tin Tin on one of his wild-
goose chases."

"Seems like he just got off shift. Didn't leave him much time
at home."

"Ain't nobody there but that shepherd dog anyways."

"His missus?"

"Gone. Run off."

"My, my," Gload said. He wagged his great head sadly. "That's
got to be tough on a young guy."

"I wouldn't spend any time feeling sorry for him. Women
don't stray unless you're not getting the job done."

"So she's taken up with somebody?"

"That's the word. She's a good-looking little gal. She needs
to be getting it somewheres." Wexler examined the backs of his
hands. "I might take a run at her myself." He favored the old
man with a vulpine leer. Gload forced a smile. He realized he
was blunting the stub of pencil, wearing a deep black hole in his
tablet.

Wexler took up Millimaki's chair and swung it around as if
he might sit in it, then reconsidered. He affected a businesslike

tone. "John, I'm taking you out today. I got your topo maps for north of the river and I want to see something come of 'em. No more dicking around."

"You're taking me out?"

"That's right. And on my own time."

"And you got maps?"

"I got maps and I want to see some fucking Xs and Os on the sonsofbitches."

"What about Millimaki? I more or less promised him I'd go on out there with him."

"Number one, he ain't here. Two, like I said before, John, I'm the ranking officer. Deputy Shitkicker made you promises he couldn't keep."

"So you're taking me out," Gload said.

"One o'clock. Have your lunch and we'll take a nice drive in the country and find some of your vics and put some poor people's minds to rest for once and for all."

"Val or no Val, I could sure use a little stretch of the legs." He pointed toward the streaked street level windows, golden with August light. "Get out in some natural sunshine."

"This ain't a picnic, John. And by the way, another snipe hunt and things might get unpleasant for you around here. Deputy Dobek has a kind of hard-on about you already. It's my fucking day off. I expect to come back with something."

"I'm just plumb grateful, Weldon," John Gload said. "I know once I get out there again it'll all come back to me."

When Wexler had gone, John Gload sat for a moment, his arm slung over the top slat of his chair. He rose and made a brief circuit of the cell, as it could only be brief, picking up in turn his accumulated wealth: a comb, a bar of soap, balled socks on a shelf. Pencil sharpener in the shape of a blue toad. He put his toothbrush in his shirt pocket, stood thinking, put it back on the shelf. Empty tablets. Magazines. Among them a John Deere dealership catalogue given him by Valentine Millimaki, which he transferred to the top of the pile. He smoothed the blanket atop his bed. Finally he sat once again. He tore loose several pages from the legal pad covered in his childish hand with smeared additions and subtractions and theoretical fields apportioned by theoretical acres, in the margins his doodlings of fabulous creatures and esoteric runes which occupied his hands while he considered perhaps the rich other-life of gentleman farmer, partnered with a father long ago frozen in the bull pines of Fergus County. He folded these neatly and buttoned them in his breast pocket and settled back to await his lunch.

SEVENTEEN

In the far west beyond the Teton Breaks, the Front Range marked the seeming edge of the world. Late August and the high cirques harbored yet crescents and stripes of snow, and in the summer haze they appeared to have been daubed on the purple-blue backcloth with a palette knife. Millimaki had arrived at the field and stood outside his sheriff's department Blazer looking out over the incalculable expanse of grain fields, much of it already cut to stubble, stretching away in all directions. They broke against the mountains like a blond sea. His father's rocky acreage had never looked like this. John Gload would have been agog.

Some small birds swarmed soundlessly in the distance. The dog sat erect in the backseat of the truck. Millimaki thought about the girl. And he remembered that ten years earlier, before he'd come on the force, a schoolteacher had been abducted and raped and left impaled on a duckfoot plow twelve miles to the east of where he stood. He wondered what in this beautiful country could inspire such evil. As if the wind that swept down from those bleak and frozen crags carried on it, like a microbe to infest the blood, the appetite of wolf and bear.

A cloud of dust appeared on the county road and he and the dog watched it approach. A sheriff's cruiser pulled in beside Millimaki's rig and a young deputy rolled down his window and said, "Just follow me. It's down the way a bit." He backed out and together they drove a half mile east and then north again and pulled through a wire gate and parked beside a small blue car.

The young man came toward Millimaki with his hand outstretched. He was taller than Millimaki and about his age. His hair beneath the Pondera County Sheriff's Department cap was an outrageous red, approaching orange, and every inch of visible skin was freckled.

"Malmberg," he said. "They call me Red."

"That's crazy," Millimaki said. "Where'd they come up with that?"

"Yeah. Go figure."

"What's with the tape?" Val said. "Must have taken about a half mile of it." The field was enclosed by yellow crime scene tape strung between cocked haphazard dowels pressed into the soil like a barrier erected by circus clowns and it snapped and fluttered and threatened to kite off on the wind.

"Yeah, no shit. I strung it myself." Malmberg pointed toward a rank of combines at the field's edge, new expensive machines with enclosed cabs, header blades with their rows of gleaming spring tines aligned. They seemed animate and rapacious and the sun turned their windshields to diamond.

"Old Farmer Brown wanted to roll in here and start to cutting. This was the only way I could keep him out. Says he's got something like a bazillion dollars sitting here and it's somebody's ass if it don't get cut more or less right away. I believe mine was the ass he was talking about. Anyways, I ain't too worried about it." He swung his arm east to west across the barley field in a papal gesture. "He ain't going to be too happy regardless." The grain was thoroughly trod, rows of parallel tracks where sheriffs and volunteers had ranged through and the ground was amber with grain as though it had been sown anew.

"We walked the whole shitteree, up and back. Nothing. Tracks go in and don't come out. Somebody thought she was picked up on that little bitty road at the end of this thing, but there ain't any tracks. Not a one. It's like she just flew away."

"What about over there?"

"It's a ditch. You got to be right on top of it to see it. There's no more than six inches of water in it now."

"Did you walk it?"

"Well, I didn't, personally, but it got walked. Like I said, it's nothing more'n a trickle. Not like you could have drownded in it."

"This her car?"

"We've been all through it."

They stood there looking. A gust came down off the Front Range and the field came alive, shuddering and undulant like a cat's back and issuing a long forlorn sigh.

"What do you think?" Millimaki said.

"I think if she'd wanted to disappear she'd had to of caught a bus and somebody or other would of seen her."

"True enough."

"If she'd wanted to disappear permanently for good she'd just as soon driven that piece of shit up there." Malmberg turned and pointed a milky and mottled hand toward the sawblade peaks. "And find a pile of brush the hell and gone. Way on up."

"That's what you'd think."

"Wouldn't you?"

"I guess most anybody with a lick of sense would."

The deputy stared long and longingly into the west. He gouged a hole in the ground with the toe of his boot, leaned and spat into it. "You know about her, right? Did they tell you?"

"Yeah, they told me," Val said. "I remember reading about it. But I didn't know all the fine points."

"She wasn't one of these bad kids. Just a kind of average girl. It was a hell of a thing. She'd grown up with every one of them kids."

"She might turn up yet, right as rain."

"A hell of a thing." The deputy went on as if he hadn't heard. "I got a twelve-year-old boy. Not much younger'n them boys that did that to her. Here after that happened for a week or so I looked at him like he might be some kind of different creature. I couldn't help it. We didn't raise him that way but still. He knew something was wrong, too. He finally just came up and got on my lap and started crying. Kids know a lot more than what you give them credit for, don't they?"

"I don't know."

"No kids?"

"No."

"You'll see," he said. "You just wait."

Malmberg's radio came to life and he went to his car. Milli-maki opened the rear door of his truck and Tom jumped down and began running his nose on the ground. He went around to sniff Malmberg's knees and the deputy tousled the dog's ears while he spoke into his mike. Val had retrieved the dog's lead and stood holding it, surveying the barley field. The wind came down and like a ventriloquist's trick the field hissed and sighed from every quarter. Malmberg came to stand beside him.

"Sorry, I got to run to town. Got a domestic." He removed his cap and ran a hand through his tangerine hair. "This son-ofabitch goes at his wife prit-near once a week. He's a first-class scumbag and so I ask myself, Why does she stay with him? He's tore hunks of hair off her head and then later in the week I see them sitting together in the café holding hands like teenagers. You ever figure that one out you let me know."

He did not wait for Millimaki to respond. He clapped one of his speckled hands on Val's shoulder, jumped into the cruiser's seat and backed onto the county road and was gone. Val stood watching the dust plume recede down the string-straight road until it disappeared beyond a low rise. All about him the barley slewed and rasped in the wind.

Because it's hard to be alone, Millimaki thought. That's what I've figured out, Red. In this country, it's just hard to be alone.

He went to the girl's car and stood looking in the window. He raised his head and looked out over the wide rolling country. Not a house or shed. Not a telephone pole. Finally he opened the door and sat in the driver's seat. He ran his hands lightly around the steering wheel. From the rearview mirror hung a tiny dream catcher and a plastic rosary. He inhaled the merest hint of perfume. "Penelope Ann Carnahan," he said. "Your name is a poem."

Reaching across he swung open the passenger side door. It squalled on a sprung hinge. He called the dog and he came and stuck his head into the car and began to snuffle at the floor-boards, the seat. He nuzzled a hooded sweatshirt in the back-seat. Millimaki held it up. On its chest, in sporadic spangles, it read ROCKSTAR. He laid it on the seat in front of the dog. "That's her, Tom-boy. That's our girl."

Beyond the ground search, the area had been flown over by a helicopter from the Air Force base at Great Falls and a stagnant reservoir had been dragged, exhuming from the murk nothing more sinister than a rotting angus heifer calf thought to have been rustled a month previous. As Malmberg had said, the girl seemed to have been lifted into the sky. It was not the first time he'd heard that or similar words when he'd shown up with the dog as the instrument of last resort, as though searchers in their desperation and despair imbued the victims with the power to rescue themselves. Changelings sprouting the wings of swallows or eagles. Angels. Transmutation by hope. He thought again of the holy card his Slovene grandmother had given him when he was a boy: The Assumption of the Virgin Mary into Heaven. He had kept it in his billfold for years, until the gilt edges were worn and the paper had become as pliable as cloth: angels with great immaculate wings escorting the Virgin toward Elysium on a stairway of feather clouds. Her face was awash with the sunlight of God. But Valentine Millimaki did not bring back angels. No, I did not, he thought. Souls did not aspire on his watch to safety or heaven but came trestled roughly from the dark woods, trapped in the alabaster statuary of rigid flesh.

The girl's track when they entered the barley was clear though some of the searchers had walked atop it. Tom surged at his lead the length of the field but then stood confused at its northernmost edge where it terminated at the narrow road Malmberg had spoken of. It was no more than parallel ruts and no vehicle had passed on it in months. Millimaki walked for a way

in the weeds at its edge. Runic tracks of birds, tracks of fox. The
dog plunged at his lead, urgent to return the way they'd come
and Val let him go. At the car once again the dog veered toward
the weedy strip beside the ditch.

"Hold on for a minute, goddamn it. Let me catch my breath."
He tied the lead to the door handle of the girl's car and the dog
whined and pawed at the dirt. Leaning against the warm quarterpanel he breathed the dusty smell of ripe grain, a scent from
his childhood. An image of his father sprang unbidden into his
head—a rare happy picture of an unhappy man, passing his
hands over the ripened heads as he walked toward the waiting
combines.

Millimaki went once again to the first tracks entering the
field, knelt and studied them: tiny feet, antic whorls of the
treads of her shoes. He got on his knees and took a long look at
one of the prints. Then he shuffled ahead on hands and knees
and studied another. And another. At last he knelt in the dirt,
his hands resting on his thighs. She had entered the barley from
the hard ground and then had carefully retraced her steps, one
footprint atop another as she backstepped from the grain field.
Now the barley tassels bowing under the wind brushed at the
flesh of Millimaki's arms. "Bright girl," he said. "Bright girl." But
he was not smiling.

Tom had torn up the ground at the limit of his lead and he
bayed crazily when he saw Millimaki emerge from the barley. He untied the leather lead and the dog nearly pulled his
arm out of the socket. "Okay, then, if you're so fucking sure."
He unsnapped the leather lead and the dog vanished in the
weeds.

A hundred yards along the ditch he came to the dog sitting,
his ears pivoting as he registered some minute sounds—the

burble of the ditch water, birdcalls, tiny things among the weed
bines. Millimaki was about to speak when he saw the plastic
straw. Later he would appreciate how very thorough she'd been.
The straw approximated as well as possible the color of the
barley and the August weed stems growing along the ditch—
thistle and hemlock, volunteer wheat. He pulled but it seemed
rooted there. He dug away at its base until the girl's lips emerged
from the dirt and he realized with a start that he was kneeling on her chest. He stood up abruptly and backpedaled, nearly
tripping over the dog. "Oh, Christ," he said. "Oh, Christ." He
stood looking down for a long while. He realized the dog was
waiting and he went to him and roughly stroked his head. He
could hardly speak. He managed, "Good, Tom," and the dog
stepped down the small incline to the ditch and lapped at the
trickle of water. Millimaki sat among the dry weeds and he sat
for a very long time. The dog came to lie at his feet. Finally
with great effort Millimaki rose and began his routine. He did
it all mechanically. He studied the ground, bent and snapped
his pictures from several angles and he stood beside the grave
turning to the four cardinal points and working the shutter—
grain fields rolling endlessly to every horizon. Then at last he
took a pair of latex gloves from his fanny pack and began to dig
the girl out. The shepherd lay with his head on his extended
forelegs, following the man's movements with his eyes.

The girl had cut away the turf in her small approximate shape
and it came away in rough squares and rectangles and then she
had dug the hole where she would lie. While breathing through
the straw she must have covered her face with loose dirt before
somehow pulling lengths of the sod over her arms, taking her
last breaths through the straw as the drugs moved slowly down
the long corridors of her veins. He was amazed at her strength

and will to leave no trace upon the earth. It must have taken her hours. Beside her in the hole were the kitchen knife and the pill bottle and she lay in it rigid and symmetrical as if composed by the hands of reverent priests. He lifted her hands each in turn, examining the torn and broken nails and turned them with difficulty to look at her palms where blisters had formed and ruptured and bled like stigmata. Millimaki brushed as much of the soil from her face as he could and with his belt knife sawed away the straw from her clenched teeth. In the end he leaned over as if he might kiss those cold lips and blew the sand from her eyelids, from the corners of her mouth.

While he waited for the coroner to make the twenty-mile trip from town, he cut away some of the crime scene tape Malmberg had taken such pains to erect and planted some of the dowels in the dirt and strung the yellow tape, defining the plot the girl had chosen for herself from the enormity of the unbearable world. She'd wanted nothing but to disappear and Millimaki and his dog had taken that from her. Soon again she would be antiseptically probed on the coroner's tray when all she had wanted in the world was to not be touched again. He would not take her picture. When he'd lifted off the turf and stood looking at her so small and pale in her grave he realized what he'd taken, what he could not put back. If the coroner wanted those pictures he could take the sonsofbitches himself.

He sat at the edge of the ditch beside her watching the red sun fall slowly behind the western rim. A meadowlark sang. Pheasant and Hungarian partridge scuttled through the field, gorging on fallen grain. He could see them come gliding in in twos and threes and flare their wings against the paling sky. He stared at the tiny jackstraw figure at his feet. There had been no angel to bear her up. In the end only numbing chemical night falling on her eyes to damp the vision of the boys in the pickup bed with their bottles and shovel handles, in the plunder of her virginity not even the warmth of a human touch.

The birds picked among the furrows like barn fowl and the barley sawed hissing above them with the wind like a breath. It was a wonderful evening. He gazed down at Penelope Carnahan. He thought about taking her hand.

Together they went up the game trail and John Gload stopped periodically to turn and take in the country as if considering their solitude in the immensity, not assuring himself of it. Wexler beside him gloomily considered the new scuffs on his boots. He ran his finger along the looping lines of the topographic map, his tongue between his lips. The map popped and fluttered in the wind and they went on. They crossed a small divide, descended into a coulee, and presently the river disappeared as did Wexler's car beside it and there was no sign whatever of the world of men on the dusty path fresh tracks of mule deer and older sign baked into the gumbo-clay like the spoor of cloven-footed prehistoric kin. In that desolate hole the wind that had raised chop on the river was a whisper and overhead a hawk drifted among the thin clouds like a harbinger, keening high and shrill.

Gload stood and made a show of locating himself and he craned his neck once to study the map Wexler held. He was a fair actor and asked if they weren't about a mile from the river and wasn't the second dam perhaps a mile downstream and Wexler turned in that direction, where the old man with his shackled hands pointed and then the chain was around Wexler's throat. The folded map fell among the weeds and the old man for leverage had his knee in the small of the younger man's back and Wexler clawed at the hands wildly, wet sounds escaping his nose and from the white grimace of his mouth and very quickly his vision began to fail and fade and in that embrace, chest to back like prison lovers, John Gload could feel the muscles in the thin frame by degrees slacken toward tranquility. He walked two paces backward and laid Wexler's body down, turned it on its side that he might maintain his grip and he held him there yet, until the sound of breath was gone, until finally he could hear the thin high call of the hawk and he let go. He looked at Wexler and smiled at the mask of dumb amazement there regarding the empty heavens and he noted the dark stain on the man's pants front. He said to him, "You weren't no surprise, Deputy. I figured there was nothing to you and I was right."

After he retrieved the shackle keys from Wexler's pocket and the clasp knife from his belt and folded away the topo map carefully so that it would not be torn or bloodied, he set his capable hands to their task. The work was difficult and even in the cool air he was shortly sweating profusely and he noted how soft he had become in the months of confinement. It felt good to take long strides down the path, and going back up with the entrenching tool from the car trunk he began to feel alive. There were tire chains kept in a burlap sack in the car's trunk and he emptied them out and brought the sack with him. The digging was easy and he made several holes—some on the bald adjacent side hills, some deep in narrow defiles plowed out by the lashing rains of spring. Some in the coulee above, some below. One he stole from a badger, the bleak hollow socket gaping from beneath a rock the size and shape of a Stonehenge monolith.

He took his time, tamping down the small holes with the
flat of the shovel and with his feet and with a sage branch he
smoothed away the tread marks of his shoes. Then he stood
back, appraising each site from different angles, different heights.
Descending, he swept the trail assiduously with the sage, bent
and shuffling like a peasant crone. By the time he reached the
car it was dusk. At the riverbank he cast several things into the
river and almost immediately the gulls began to swarm and
screech. He stooped and put a round rock in the sack and threw
it far out into the chop and then he washed his hands and arms
and shoes as best he could in the silty water. The gulls splashed
and dove and with his hands pressed against his ears John
Gload stood on the rocky riverbank for several minutes watching. Though they were for him malign and detestable they
were nonetheless a facet of his dream and they conjured for
him the plowed fields of his youth. He was suddenly very tired.
Oh how I could sleep right now, he thought. Oh how I could
sleep.

The gulls came off the river and like the birds of his childhood memories began to home in on ground he had recently
turned in the hills above. His thoughts of sleep were prurient
and he turned his burning eyes toward the sun, low and molten
in the west. Oh, yes, he would sleep. One errand and he would
sleep indeed.

By the time the coroner had come and gone Millimaki was too
tired to make the return drive, at the end of which was his empty
cabin with its fire grate of cold ash and a refrigerator provisioned
with little else but beer. He took a room in the town, ate his dinner at a truck stop where his companions were long-haul driv-

ers sitting alone and catatonic in plastic booths, their harlequin eyes to the black window glass watching comets burn bleakly through the night on the interstate toward Canada. Wherever Millimaki looked he saw the girl's dirty face, the image like a photographic negative seared into the back of his eyeballs. He went back to lie on his sterile bed in a room that smelled of stale smoke. The dog when he came in rose to nuzzle his hand and returned to the bed he'd made in the worn brown shag.

Millimaki lay for half an hour squeezing his eyes against the shards of crimson neon penetrating the dusty draperies through lacerations that seemed to have been made with a knife. He got up, dressed, and went into the warm night and down the lone illuminated street of the deserted town. It was summer yet but soon the wind scouring the neglected asphalt and rustling the leaves in the infrequent box elder trees seemed to bear for him some message from the distant high snowfields. He turned up the collar of his coat. The swaying lamplights made a strange parade of jittering light pools through which Millimaki walked, encountering not a living creature afield.

He trudged numbly past near-identical single-room houses sided with asphalt brick and trailers set upon ill-aligned cinder blocks all but encased in snarls of hemlock and rampant lilacs and soon beneath his feet the pavement gave way to gravel. Coyotes bayed from the bluffs rising darkly to the west of town, the stream weaving beneath them at that time of year little but a series of tepid pools and brackish plaits burbling from the tangled willows with the sound of muffled voices. There was no moon and as he passed beyond the last town lights it was if he had passed through a portal, from the civilized world to one where darkness prevailed. He stopped in the road and held up his hands against the sky as if he might sift the stars in their billions through his fingers and make sense of the equivocal black like an ancient pyromancer. He walked for a long time. Trash fluttered along the right-of-way fence. Near a culvert where the creek went beneath the road he sat down in the wild ditch weeds. Small things scurried away and then he could hear nothing but a muted electric hum the wind elicited from the fence wires.

The girl's face again appeared before him and there were others, emancipated to float free and wide in that great black dome—porcelain masks of winter's victims, the drowned, sallow and bulbous, staring unperturbed from the stout embrace of submerged trees. Dismantled Picasso faces grinning crookedly from a bed of talus stones. There, too, was the blue-black mask his mother wore. The painted kewpie face of his recurrent dream was another lie, more deceit. Because it was not white and smooth but a bulging swollen thing above the rope with a half inch of black tongue that the flies had found. He put his face in his hands. After a few minutes he said the girl's name aloud—Penelope Ann Carnahan—like a prayer or a conjuring, the exquisite beauty of her resolve a searing indictment of his shitty pathetic loneliness and self-pity. At home, in a closet, Glenda's shirts and dresses hung like cartoon ghosts and only a day ago he had pressed his face into them, breathing her faint perfume and dampening the fabric like a child. He was ashamed.

Once they had hiked to the top of the eastern flank of the Big Snowies and they could see from there five mountain ranges, blue and isolate in seas of emerald spring grass. In the southeast, toward the Musselshell, antelope it seemed for sheer joy of speed coursed among the sagebrush and in the north a great cloud hove up, as white and substantive as a massif thrust up new from the prairie. She stood for several minutes turning, with her hand visoring her eyes, and finally put her arm around him and thanked him for all of it. As though it were a gift he had given her.

They ate their lunch atop a colossal lichened outcrop, which lay above the grass like the barnacled back of a whale and he told her about his uncle who had brought a Dutch woman home from the war and the marriage had lasted less than a year. When as a boy he'd asked about it his uncle had said simply, "It just didn't take."

"What, like it was a grapevine?" she asked.

"Those were the words. I don't know. I was something like ten years old."

"Well, to continue the metaphor, Valentine, he must not have made a good bed for it."

And he thought now, what bed had he made for his own wife? A four-room cabin at the end of a bad road. Twelve hundred a month and an eleven-year-old Datsun and lodgepole pine to heat her house. That was the bed he'd made. A red-hot oven and flies on the windowsill and a half-warped door drift-locked half the winter mornings and boots caked with impossible gumbo from an impassable road. Him, with his murderous companion and his lousy fucking twelve hundred a month and a graveyard shift. And his retinue of dead—like family, she had said. Or like lovers.

In his farmboy credulousness he had thought he could take her from the ivied trellises and green lawns of Dublin, Ohio, and make her happy with his mere fidelity. And she had starved on it, like a dog in a kennel with a bone alone for sustenance. Whatever there was left of himself he had given to the dead. She was right—the dead were easier. Like Penelope Carnahan, silent and beautiful in her eternal and seductive slumber.

The wind by the time he roused himself and began his walk back had come in earnest. Grit scoured from the bluffs stung his face like spoondrift, and tumbleweeds bowled past making clattering skeletal sounds in the blackness. He went before the gusts down the dark road with his arms outspread. His heart lay in his chest like a ballast stone and he thought that if not for that, he might kite away weightless and insubstantial as the feed sacks and bale-twine boxes pilloried to the fence wires.

She climbed the metal stairs in her practical shoes which, by shift's end, seemed cobbled from stone. The wind skirled weirdly in the stairwell and trash flew about like vile birds and flapped and lodged among the metal balusters. She paused on the landing to catch her breath and when he appeared the old man wore a look of mild surprise. The wind blew his thin hair forward and he swept it back with a huge hand. She didn't remember seeing him there before and wondered if he was someone's father or grandfather. The wind swept the thin strands of hair across his face again and he held them back, his hand at his forehead in a strange salute. He stood for a moment on the stairs two steps above her and she smiled at him but he only stared, cocking his head, his expression mildly thoughtful, and then he went past her and she could hear his heavy tread on the metal stairs, marking his descent by the pong pong pong of the treads. The sound stopped somewhere short of the ground floor and she stood listening as did he and then she could hear his tread again and she hurried to her door along the walkway dimly illuminated by the globed halogens in the adjacent parking lot. She was horrified she'd forgotten to lock the apartment's door and when she stepped inside she turned the thumb lock on the knob and threw

home the deadbolt and slid the security chain into its track and
for reasons she couldn't name stood breathless with her ear to
the door for a full minute.

Through the parted blinds she watched the parking lot,
weirdly blanched at that late hour beneath the buzzing lamps.
Beyond the rows of cars she thought she saw the old man ambling
slowly along the green boulevard or it may have been someone
else or perhaps it was only her weary eyes at that late hour concocting from the windy shadows of the arborvitae a fairy-tale
ogre shuffling his dirty brogans toward some far-off lair festooned
with bones.

In the room again he lay with his fingers laced behind his head.
Ribbons of ruby light shone through the rents in the curtains
and lay across his legs like angry sutures. He'd been awake for
nearly twenty-four hours and had walked nearly ten miles on
the gravel in the dark and yet he could not sleep. He sat up on the
edge of the bed. The television strobed. Women in scant clothing humped and churned to a manic Latin beat and there was
much excited talk about abs and buns. He clicked it off.

He sat for several minutes immobile as a stone, the primary-
color efflux of the television like a flashbulb still erupting in his
vision. When he'd left that day after talking to the sheriff he'd
stopped at the mailbox and gathered up the mail and put it on
the dashboard of the truck. There'd been catalogues and bills
and Glenda's magazines redolent of feminine scent. And there'd
been a letter from his sister which now stood against the base
of the bedside lamp. He picked it up and turned it over and over
and in the end set it back. He could not take her PS tonight. It
may not be this letter or the next but he felt eventually it would
come: "PS—Why did you dawdle on the road?" "Why did you

stand there and eat an apple?" "Why," at last, "did you not save her?"

Though the room seemed already warm, the wall heater unaccountably clicked on and stale air rolled across the room, conjuring out of the vile shag, with its smell of cigarettes and sweet perfumes, a desolate history of quick and forbidden couplings. Tom raised his head from his bed and looked at the heater and looked at the man and lay back. Nearby Millimaki's holstered .357 hung on a chairback, its bluing sultry and inviting. Suddenly he remembered what he'd heard about Ed Teagarden—thirty-two years in the department, happily married, had taken a shotgun to his garage and inhaled a load of #6 upland game shot, the sudden inutility of unwanted retirement harvesting fruit from the garden of his secret dystopia. It blossomed outlandishly on the wall above his workbench.

Millimaki fished through his wallet until he found the number written on the back of a receipt. A woman's voice came on an answering machine and began to talk. He hung up and called again. And again.

Finally a voice said, "Don't you not get it, asshole. It's three-fifteen in the morning. I'll get the cops on your ass."

"Jean, I'm sorry. It's Val."

"Oh, Val." He could hear her exhale, and the timbre of her voice when she spoke again was soft and sympathetic. "She's not here. I think she went out on a Life Flight. There was an accident in the Highwoods. I think the Highwoods. Somewhere out there. I thought she would be home by now."

"What was that about the cops? Is everything all right?"

"I'm fine. I can't sleep. I thought someone had been in the apartment."

"Lock the door."

"There was a man. It was nothing. The wind blowing and my imagination going crazy over nothing."

"I'm out of town. I could have someone come by."

"No, that's okay."

"I could get them to send a car by."

"How are you, Val?"

"I can't sleep, either. I haven't slept it seems like for a year."

"You can get something for that."

"I know. I hate taking anything."

"Val, that's not where she is."

"You mean the Life Flight."

"You could probably have checked on that. Checked if there was an accident."

"I'm really tired, Jean."

"I mean you could have that checked. With your department."

"Sure. I could. Why would I?"

"Val, that's not where she is."

"She's not out on the Life Flight."

"Yes. That's not right. I can't say anything more." She exhaled deeply into the receiver—a liquid sigh laden with weariness and all the heart-cracking mundane sorrow of her profession. "It just won't do any good anyway."

"Jean," he said. "Jean?"

EIGHTEEN

He'd made no attempt to hide the car though the uncut ditch weeds when he'd driven it off the road rose above the fenders and little could be seen of it but the roof and windows. There was much to do and the old man gathered pencil and paper and started in immediately, pacing deliberately down the narrow orchard lane that led to his house. He paced and stopped to scribble in a small wide-ruled notebook and paced again. To his right the scraggly orchard, where songbirds flitted and chirruped softly and on his left the old right-of-way fence whose strands of rusted wire hung in low bights or lay hopelessly garbled on the ground among the weeds. Beyond it acres of parched sage, running to the breaks of the river and into the low hills dotted in that arid place with random tortured junipers and bull pine. Pace, stop, write. Turn, pace. He consulted the sun, the shadows of the trees upon the ground. He noted the direction of the wind and with his head erect and eyes closed he appeared to be taking the scent of something. At last he stopped and turned in a circle, made a final notation with the stub of pencil and then, like a child who'd tired of a game, walked from the midst of tangled trees and through the weedy ditch toward the house.

At his table he transcribed his notes onto a larger sheet of paper, the pencil stub scraping slow and painfully along the page. He sat back and examined the work for a long moment then crumpled it and began again on a second sheet. By the fifth page he was satisfied. He held it at arm's length. He set it down and stood back and looked at it from a distance. He walked around the table and looked at it from several angles with a squinted eye.

Beneath the sink he found a coffee can Francie had used for compost waste. He took it to the back-door stoop and put in the note pad and the failed drawings and at last even the pencil and burned it all, the flames a comfortable orange in the velvet blue light of dusk. Nighthawks as he stood over the guttering can flared above the apple trees against a rose sky. A distant squall was prophesied on the breeze by the smell of wet sage. When the can had cooled he took it up and bore it like a monstrance before him down the lane where he trod the ashes into the dirt. He flattened the can under his heavy shoes and sailed it far out into the brush. The day's last sunrays gleamed on the rear window of Wexler's car, dangerously atilt in the borrow ditch of the county road. While the nighthawks veered and swooped above him he stood listening. If it was the end, and it almost certainly was, he had set things right. He felt a kind of peace he'd not known for years, since he was a boy. The day was done, the field plowed.

He turned then and went through the ditch and wove among the trees, no longer counting his steps now because they were counted and recorded and archived and he sat with his back against a tree under the dangling harrow tines in the mild evening air until it was quite dark.

"Some kid out sighting in his aught-6 found Wexler. Or his dog did. Part of him. The dog found part of Wexler. It was just a damn accident."

"Oh, God."

"God only knows where the rest of him is. Buried out there with his other bones. Or in the river. I don't know. We got the dogs out, boats in the water." The sheriff paused, swiveled his chair to the window. "He did his old best number on him."

Val sought a chair and sat unbidden. The sheriff swiveled back, considered him with weary eyes over the rim of his reading glasses.

"You know when they found him he was just sitting in a chair out at his place like he was waiting for a cab."

"I know."

"Just like the first time. Didn't make a bit of fuss. Put out his hands for the bracelets, said howdy boys."

Val looked into his palms. He could feel the sheriff's eyes on him.

"Then he asked where was Deputy Millimaki."

Val said nothing.

"Said he was expecting Millimaki. Said he'd like to talk to the deputy."

"I can't explain that."

"I'm not asking you to."

"He won't tell me where Wexler is, if that's what you mean."

"I'm sure he won't. That's another secret John Gload will take to his grave. And by Christ I hope he takes it there soon."

"Yessir. I hope so."

The sheriff removed his half-glasses and set them deliberately on his desk atop its chaos of papers. He passed his hands across his face in a washing motion. When he looked up, his eyes were fond and enormously sad. "Do you in point of fact, Val? Do you hope that?"

That question Millimaki considered as he drove home that afternoon and it occupied his thoughts all that evening as he sat on his porch watching the sky dim and the stars emerge from the void with their vanguard of bats and he even had the opportunity to discuss the difficult matter later with Weldon Wexler when he appeared in Millimaki's dream. But Wexler, carrying an armload of bloodless limbs like stovewood and wearing a vivid carmine scar on his neck, was disinclined to speak.

John Gload in the month of October was convicted of first-degree murder and was to spend the rest of his life in the Montana State Penitentiary in Deer Lodge. A casualty of the strenuous proceedings, his lawyer succumbed finally to the ravages of his vice and had been committed to a detoxification center in Billings. He'd shown up for trial in the suit he'd slept in, his bald dome white as an egg beneath the lights, and his tremors would not allow him to open his briefcase or lift a glass of water to his cracked and spluttering lips. John Gload accepted this as an inevitability and seemed hardly to notice.

Gruesome photographs and mock-ups of the young man disinterred from his unsatisfactory grave in the Breaks were set upon easels at the front of the courtroom and the heart surgeon for two long hours explicated them, in his thousand-dollar suit parading up and back like a university don, poking and slapping

at the exploded images with a wooden pointer. He described
the damage to the heart and how the chest must be accessed for
its repair and at last setting aside the pointer and weaving his
gracile fingers through the air like a tailor or shoemaker he illus-
trated his method for wiring together the sternum where it had
been split. A technique unlike any other, he said. Unique. Proprietary. The prosecuting attorneys rolled their eyes at one another
discreetly and Gload's young public defender stammered his
objections. Even so, Gload had been intensely interested. He
was at that time seventy-seven years old. Sidney White, in view
of his cooperation, at an earlier date had been given forty years,
ten suspended. His place of incarceration was yet to be deter-
mined. It was thought he should not inhabit the same institu-
tion as John Gload. White's trial for the Miles City rape and
assault was pending. Regardless, he would be nearly the age of
his mentor before he resumed his short and inglorious career in
the world of free men.

NINETEEN

He went slowly along a long gray corridor, the redoubtable masonry of clammy stone on either side stacked and mortared against the penetration of hope. The familiar smell of disinfectant and floor wax was in his nostrils, the walls lined with scarred wooden benches with high backs that may have been pews rescued from a desanctified church. In passing he read names carved into the seats circumscribed with hearts or conjoined with chains and there were admonitions in crude calligraphy to fuck off, to eat shit. In one high seat back an optimistic vandal had inscribed his assurance that Millimaki would be reborn. The work of feral children, of wives and lovers mutely enraged by their celibacy, their infidelities. Mothers had dug their nails into the soft wood as they waited in the dank corridor to see the fruit of their wombs turned out so briefly from their cages.

The familiar fluorescents as he walked cast their antiseptic light. Another sally gate slid open with a rasp of metal and shortly, on his right, through the scratched and foggy Plexiglas he saw the face of John Gload, more equine now, the long jaw bones prominent, his eyes seemingly grown larger. All else save his hands seemed diminished and he sat with them flat on the table, sphinxlike, staring vacantly into the glass before him, heedless of the clamor of voices and the scrape of chairs. The terrible light turned his skin to marble. Several small round Band-Aids adorned his forehead and neck, the spurious flesh color like mismatched patches on a creased and faded shirt.

"My, my," he said. "Deptee." His smile revealed now a dead tooth the color of oak. "You're looking good."

"Hello, John. How they treating you?"

"Treat me like a goddamn convict, is what they do."

"If the shoe fits."

Gload stared frankly at the younger man's face for a long uncomfortable moment and then grinned once again, the awful canine like a grub clinging to his smile.

"Did I ever tell you that in the old days they used to put concrete shoes on these assholes who tried to escape? Weighed twenty pounds. Had to wear them shoes every waking hour, walking around clank clank clank. Like that."

"No, I guess you didn't."

"Well, it's a fact." He removed his cigarettes from a breast pocket and laid them in front of him, aligning the pack fastidiously with the table edge. He coughed. His voice had more gravel in it. "So you're a fed now, is that it?"

Millimaki shook his head in amazement. "Still tapped into your jailbird pipeline. You're a goddamn wonder."

The old man made motions as if to snatch feathers swirling around his head. "Words float around, Val, and you pick them up."

"Amazing. Any word out there regarding the color of my shorts?"

Gload effected a mirthless smile, the parchment skin of his horse's jaw tight. His tongue worried at the dead tooth. He said, "Please tell me you ain't FBI at least."

"ATF. About two years now."

"All Those Fuckers. If you'll pardon me. It's just a joke, Val."

"I hadn't heard that one," Millimaki lied. "That's not bad."

Gload removed a cigarette from his pack and tapped an end on his thumbnail. He said, "I appreciated that picture you sent."

"I took that on my last search. I was clearing out some stuff. Thought you might like it."

"Nice picture," he said. "Never did find the letter went with it, though."

"I'm not much of a letter writer."

The old man studied his hands and the burning cigarette between his fingers. "Kind of thought you might of stopped by and say good-bye before they shipped me out."

"They put me on two weeks' leave after that. You were gone by the time I got back. Then I got this gig and, well, on to other things."

"Well, anyways." Gload looked up. A weary smile, his lips thin and chapped. "They must treat you good. You're looking better'n the last time I seen you. Eating good, getting more sleep, am I right? Making good money?"

"I'm doing okay, John. And what about you? How you making it?"

The old man was terribly thin and bent. The signs of his chronic insomnia were very much in evidence—even through the hazy plastic barrier Millimaki noted the old man's eyes latticed with veins, the skin beneath them dark as war paint. His hand when he reached for his cigarettes exhibited a faint quaver.

"Oh, not what you might say thriving. I don't sleep much. You know how it is. Just living it out, like I told you once. Living it out." He struck his lighter to the end of a filterless Camel and blew smoke at the ceiling. "We're like two trains going different ways, Val."

"What about that farming dream?"

He snorted. "That gets harder and harder. Just like an old tattoo—the color has begun to fade and sometimes I can't hardly see it no more." He paused and wanly smiled. "Except for them gulls. Sonsofbitches are clear as ever."

He sat smoking. In the adjacent cubicle a man began to shout in Spanish and pound the tabletop and the glass in front of him with the flat of his hand. He jumped to his feet and his chair lurched backward to the floor. Two guards moved toward him. He was led away in cuffs weeping. Beside Millimaki, beyond the insubstantial privacy barrier, a young woman sat in the chair as rigid as an obelisk, her hands covering her face. John Gload seemed to notice nothing. He had lifted his ashtray with the cigarette in it from the tabletop that it not be disturbed and when the man was taken away set it down.

"You speak that lingo?" he said.

"Not much."

"He was asking her to save him. That's a good one. Oh save me." He did not look as the young man was drug away or at the girl beyond the glass but examined his cigarette or perhaps he considered the troubling phenomenon of its quivering end because he wore a wistful look. Finally the old man said, "So you were in the neighborhood?"

"Something like that," Millimaki said. "I got your letter. You understand I couldn't just come right away."

"I wasn't going nowheres." By way of illustrating this fact he half turned in his chair and nodded toward a uniformed guard who stood sleepily in front of a door with wire running through the glass. He turned back, shaking his head.

Millimaki said, "I always have wondered, John, why you didn't leg it out after Wexler. Why you waited out there."

"The damnedest thing you should ask that, Valentine." The old man wore a thin smile. "I'm just getting to that in a way."

"So what's on your mind, John?"

Gload adjusted the ashtray a half inch nearer, turned it on the tabletop which told in its gouges a hundred-year history of wrist chains. "I told you about a lot of things, Val, in those months we had together and I know you passed some of the shit on to the Bull and I do not hold that against you in the very least because I know it's your job. Was your job, anyways. But I'm going to tell you one last thing and I need your promise before I do. Your word that this is just between you and me."

"How in hell can you ask a promise of me after all that's happened?"

"Because we're friends, Val, aren't we? Can you sit there and deny that we're friends?"

"I don't know what we are."

"Friends, by God. Friends is what we are."

"John, I don't know if you can be friends with somebody who you think might cut your throat if the opportunity arose."

"Valentine," Gload said. He said the young man's name with a long exhalation, like a sigh. He passed one hand down his forehead and rubbed at his inflamed eyes. For a full minute, as Millimaki shifted on his chair, the old man sat with his hands cupped to his ears as if he would shut out further lies, further hurt.

Finally he rose up and spoke. "Think about this, Deputy. I want you to think about the times we were alone together and it was the same thing with that Wexler asshole. It was the same thing. It was nothing for me to get him. Think about how many times we stood out there in that park full of trees in the dark and there wasn't nobody around and you turned your back on me. Just like Wexler did. Many many times. Twenty or thirty. A hundred times. That many times I could of got hold of you. So, yes, friends is what I think we are."

"Is that how it happened? With Wexler?"

"I don't want to talk about that on account of I don't want you to be thinking about it for the rest of your life. I wouldn't do that to you. Val, I got a lot of feelings for you."

"Friendship, then, because you didn't kill me."

His tired eyes stared into Millimaki's. "It does not, Deputy, get truer than that."

"What's the promise, John? I can't promise you anything without hearing it."

"You won't have to do nothing for a while. I don't know how long but not for a while."

"What is it?"

"I want you to claim me when I cash in and to bury my ashes."

"For Christ sake, I can't do that. That's something your family does."

"Now you know good and goddamn well I don't have nobody. I told you all that."

"There's got to be somebody. Hell, Francie. Your wife. Francie."

"Gone."

"She'd come back for something like that."

"She's not coming back, Val, that's the thing. Or maybe I should say she never left. That's why I never kited out."

"I don't even know what the hell that means. In any case, when it does happen, the state takes care of that. Down on the prison farm I think. I could check on that."

"No."

"I can't do it."

"In my orchard with no stone or nothing. All's you need to do is to dig a hole."

"I can't."

"You can, too. A simple hole in the ground. And here's the deal. I can pay you for your troubles."

"You're not paying me because I can't do it."

"Val, I've checked into all this. I'm about a half jailhouse lawyer after all these years in and out of such places."

"Has to be next of kin or nobody."

"Well, yes. I done that."

"What?"

"You're my next of kin, Val."

"I am no such thing."

"Well, you're a few years behind the times, Deputy. They don't call it that anymore. They call it 'appointing a personal representative.' But it's the same thing. I prefer the sound of 'next of kin' because it's, you know, more familiar. But it's a what-you-call bygone term. And so I done that and I made a holographic will and a devisee. Which is you, Valentine."

Millimaki stared openmouthed at the old killer, who favored him through the Plexiglas with a smile so tranquil he seemed a different Gload altogether.

"This is crazy."

"Devisee is like an heir."

"This would take years."

"It's all set up and legal as God."

"I won't do it."

Gload turned his attention to the Camel on the ashtray, shaping its end with great care and nodding his head as though in affirmation of something. To Millimaki's left the young Mexican woman sat yet, ashen and immobile as a caryatid, her eyes reflecting an emptiness beyond the chair where her husband had so recently sat, in those black portals an unreckonable vacancy cold as far space where tears could neither form or fall. She was very small and seemed more waiflike still when she rose, passing a mesmerized Millimaki with steps so deliberate it was as if her bones were of frailest glass, and she left in her wake a scent of springtime blooms.

John Gload watched him watch. He waited for Millimaki to turn once more to the glass.

"Here it is then, Val. I was hoping I wouldn't have to play my hole card. That you'd do this for me out of pure friendship." He leaned toward the barrier and opened the collar of his workshirt, revealing among the sparse gray hairs a tiny silver chain, tight as a choker, girdling the leathery wattle of his neck. The silver dolphin nestled at the hollow of his throat.

Millimaki stared in disbelief.

"This was my other gift to you, Deputy Millimaki. I gave you your life in a manner of speaking and that's something. And I gave you hers, too. I could of took it but I chose to give it. Lots of times since I thought I should of took it because she caused you a lot of pain and it hurt me to see you thataway, it truly did. I thought about it for quite a long time, Val. I remember doing it real clear. I sat in that car for a long time, thinking about what would be the best thing to do for Valentine Millimaki, my friend. And I still do think about it. And then I ask this little tiny favor of you and you say you can't do it. You say you won't." His terrible eyes bore through the Plexiglas. "Tell me how that's right, Valentine. Tell me how that's anywheres near fair."

Millimaki could only stammer. "How?"

"How what?"

"Did you find her? Get that close?"

"A couple of phone calls, a couple of little white lies. It took nothing, Val. I got talents. You never really allowed that."

Millimaki could scarcely find his voice. "You went in her place? Her apartment?"

The old man's head drooped wearily, the years with their burden and the memories of difficult decisions settling at that instant like a great stone upon the knuckled bones of his neck. He ground out his cigarette, rolled his ravaged eyes up to Millimaki. He said, "I don't know that I have a thing you'd call a soul, Val, but I recanize it in other people. You have such a thing. I seen it smudged across your face the very first time I seen you. So I know you'll do this thing for me. Just put me up there next to Francie."

"Christ, it was Jean. It was Glenda's roommate you saw that night."

Gload stared blandly through the barrier. "It don't matter."

"I called that night. Christ, Jean saw you. It wasn't Glenda."

"All that don't matter, Val. I could of got her, one way or the other."

"And you got the chain then."

"Don't be a fucking cop now when I need you, Val. I'm asking you, just put me up there next to Francie."

"Where? Up where?"

"In the orchard. That's where she is. And that's where I'm going to be, too."

"Your wife's in the orchard?" Millimaki said. "On your place?"

But the old man did not hear, had retreated to his haven in the Breaks and his ears were filled with the sound of wind in the untended trees and the flutter of the songbirds that resided there. His eyes, gorged red blossoms dyed with the blood he had spilled on the world, stared beyond Millimaki's head and beyond the unassailable stones and wire and the desolate prison town.

"In the apple trees," he said.

TWENTY

John Gload had been in the state penitentiary for five and a half years and in that time his insomnia never left him. He was eighty-two years old. He accepted his age and that the elderly seldom slept well and considering that even as a younger man he had never slept, it was little surprise to him. But he had his trickery to fool it and at times it still worked. Perhaps this night. He lay on his narrow cot, the muted noises of the prison gallery in his ears—the snores and moans, the drone of the high suspended lights that were a curse in every joint he had ever been in, the maddening slow drip of the faulty showerheads down the corridor that seemed somehow as the night deepened to grow louder, at this desolate hour clanging like rivets on the concrete floor.

Beneath his bunk are two issues of *Successful Farming*. Taped to the cinder-block wall above his head the photograph of a field sent to him years ago by Valentine Millimaki—endless ripe

grain and a slash of chalk sky adorned with a single bird of indeterminate species. In the photograph the bird is very small. In
the uncertain enormity one could not tell its size in the actual
world. It may have been vulture or crow or sparrow. In one
corner of the picture is an unfocused yellow banner with black
printed words which he cannot make out. On a paintless metal
shelf in the cell a few swollen paperback books without covers,
a comb and nail clippers, a yellow legal pad at a folding desk.

He lay on his narrow cot thinking about the field. And in
the field are things as familiar to him as his own face—the red
kits outside their den; far-off butte tops, phantasmal in the summer heat-haze; roiling grasshoppers spinning from under the
tires; the gulls. He went around the field, once, twice. And then
the bull Doogan came by and shone his light and he was forced
to begin again. The guard's footfalls receded, the saffron light
dimming, fading, gone. He took hold of the tractor's ladder rail
once again and placed his foot on the first rung but he could not
pull himself up. He lay thinking, Damn, boy, lift your foot, one
two three. But he could not move. The summer sun bore down
and he saw his boot on the rung and his hand on the rail and
the gulls came planing in, circling down and down and down
until like summer insects they swarmed about his head. He
could not raise a hand to warn them off nor could he call out
and the cries that had haunted him awake and asleep for over
seventy years drown out everything.

Guard Gerald Doogan carries in his belly a constant pain which
he thinks is surely an ulcer and he walks down the row with his
hands on his tender stomach in the posture of women who are
several months pregnant. He worries about his young daughter
who spends her evening hours in her room alone with the Vir-

gin Mother and he worries about his wife whose joints are swollen and tender to the touch. In these cages are boys little older than his only child who have settled with blood disputes over vials of powder made from cold medicine and fertilizer and he worries about a world where such things happen. His daughter's room is lit with candles and she prays on her knees in this dim place for hours. It wouldn't hurt you to say a rosary, thinks Doogan. It has been years.

He pauses outside a cell to remove an antacid tablet from his pocket where he carries them by the dozen like coins and he chews it woodenly while lighting a cigarette. He shines his light into the cell. John Gload lies on his side with his back to the hallway and he shifts slightly, as though the beam of light possesses substance—heat or cold or movement, like wind.

Guard Doogan goes down the row. He stops to throw his cigarette in one of the toilets. The water in the bowl runs without stopping and the showerheads weep and spatter on the concrete.

He lights another cigarette and smokes and thinks of his wife with her poisoned joints and of his daughter and then he turns to retrace his steps, a route he has walked five thousand nights. He imagines his Wellingtons have worn a trough in the concrete walkway and he tells his wife this as a matter of fact: I have worn a trough with my boots in the floor. He flashes his light into the old man's cell once again and the cone of light illuminates an empty bunk, a hanging blanket. He shines it toward the cell's toilet and sees nothing and thinks for an illogical instant that John Gload is gone. He swings the light back and then sees the old man beneath his bunk. He calls to him, says, "Gload, get up from there," but the old man does not move and does not move, says, "Get up, old man."

————

He sits high on the spring seat and the tractor churns through the dirt and the polished disks are small brilliant suns themselves, turning the soil in long slow serpents. The river in the distance is a shimmering knife blade and when he passes, the foxes raise their heads and follow with their anthracite eyes the young Gload on his perch and he feels the thrum of the engine in his bones, like the beat of the heart of the earth.

EPILOGUE

From the grassy side yard as he walked around the house a covey of Hungarian partridge flushed, sailing beyond the apple trees. Once above the leafy topmost branches they simply turned their compact bodies and set their wings and the wind took them out of sight in an eyeblink. Though he'd only been there once and that nearly eight years ago, from his many discussions with John Gload the place seemed familiar to him. He noted its disrepair, the slow decrepitude occasioned by the long vacancy since Gload's imprisonment. Clapboards hung loose from the walls and copper gutters sagged in perilous loops from the peeling fascia. All along the bellying soffit, hornets' nests hung like sinister fruit. Beside the back door a wooden chair, the dowels loose in their sockets, seat split and splintery from rain and sun and snow. He stood there and imagined the man whose ashes he carried biding the evening cool. The garden a tangle of weeds, strangled blooms throbbing with bees, and four enormous sunflowers leaned above the chaos, forlorn and druidical in their shabby attire.

The screen door stood ajar, badly warped and canted from Dobek's rough treatment when they'd first come for Gload those years ago and it made faint bird sounds as it rocked in the breeze. The door of the house was locked but he was able to push back the latch with his pocketknife blade so loose did it fit in the jamb. The door opened onto the kitchen, the linoleum there covered with a fine grit as if someone had recently sanded it for dancing. It displayed evidence of a brisk commerce of mice and packrats. Millimaki stooped to pick up a woman's handkerchief from the floor but it proved to be only a paper napkin, its edges made curious and asymmetrical lace by tiny teeth. Curtains shifted as the wind insinuated itself through the shrunken sash sides and the brass rings on their rods clattered softly. The house creaked and moaned. The loose clapboards made a strange fluttering sound beneath a gust of wind like a deck of riffled cards.

He went from room to room and found himself at last standing over the bed John Gload had shared with the woman he had called his wife. It was situated beneath a window and lay in a quadrangle of sallow light. He stared out the glass at the apple trees. An ashtray sat on the dusty sill. He set the metal canister down on the mattress and sat beside it and it toppled with a sound of shifting sand. A faint dust rose from the coverlet. He looked around the room. A chest of drawers, a calendar picturing a small yellow bird. In the gloom of a closet he could make out a row of paired and neatly aligned women's shoes that might have been a rank of elderly aunts hiding in that dim place in the moments before a surprise party, gloved hands pressed to their painted lips.

On a shelf in the garden shed as foretold he found the rusted Bag Balm can with its folded paper and he found the digging tools and he toted all down the road, so long unused it was now merely two paths separated by a windrow of wild wheat that sang on the undercarriage of his rented car when he'd arrived. He carried the spade and the spud bar over one shoulder and the canister cradled in his elbow and the dust rose beneath his feet like talcum. At the beginning of the inroad where he'd parked he stopped and leaned the tools against the car's quarterpanel and fished in his shirt pocket for the map. He unfolded it on the hood of the car, staring down at the old killer's rude cartography, his juvenile script. He felt like a child on a treasure hunt.

With his heels in the gravel at the edge of the county road he began pacing. And counting. He counted one hundred five steps ("normal steps, just regular walking steps") and stopped. There beside the road a great red stone stuck above the weeds. He had no idea of its size. It may well have had its roots in hell but what he could see of it would have weighed six or eight hundred pounds. It was cracked so perfectly in half it looked to have been cut with a band saw and it was here Millimaki was instructed to turn ninety degrees east and enter the orchard trees.

It was an awkward business, holding the childish map and the digging implements and the canister containing the ashes of the old killer. The fallen apples crushed beneath his feet gave off a winey smell as he counted his paces through the weft of branches and the knee-deep grass that grew thick among the gray boles of the trees. But Gload had been meticulous and had rehearsed the process many times against confusion and in ten minutes' time Millimaki nearly walked into the suspended harrow tines that marked where her bones were planted.

There was nothing there to indicate that a hole had been dug. The grass had grown up and the trees had dropped their leaves year upon year and the neglected apples moldered in the dirt. He began to dig and despite notations on the map's border assuring him that Francie's bones lay some six feet down, he feared with each shovelful that he would run the spade into a leg bone or dredge into the light instead of one of the innumerable rocks a grinning skull bewigged with auburn hair.

The day was mild and the wind found him even in that sheltered place but he was soon sweating nonetheless. Smooth round rocks from that ancient riverbed clanged under the spade's blade and roots as obdurate as reinforcing bar appeared and he chopped at them until his hands burned. He stopped once and laid his jacket aside in the grass and resumed digging. When the hole was three feet deep he stopped. It was less a grave than a posthole, like so many he had dug in the poor soil of his father's dryland operation under the buffalo jump. He leaned the spade and the metal bar in the crotch of a tree and ran a sleeve across his forehead. Above the faint rattle of dry leaves he thought he heard a cry but he stood listening and there was nothing. For an instant clear as crystal the far metronomic rofe rofe rofe of a dog. Then nothing. In the higher branches beyond the reach of deer a few small apples hung tenaciously on among the leaves, desiccated red gourds like Christmastime ornaments that seemed out of place among the gnarled phalanges of the feral trees—gray limbs, pale grass, pale sky.

When he tipped the can into the hole he was surprised at the rasping sound it made. He reversed the shovel and with the handle stirred among the ashes. He lay down and put his face close to be sure. Dust rose in the hole. A root cellar smell. Ashes, bits of charred bone. Finally he reached into the cool maw and sifted the mixture through his fingers but there were no teeth. He stood and wiped John Gload's ashes in a pale gray smear on his pants. It occurred to him that the old man would have approved of the exquisite anonymity of his own grave. Perhaps after all it was his plan—devout practitioner of his craft even at the end.

Millimaki stood looking down into the hole. After a while he removed Gload's last letter from the snap-button pocket of his shirt. He smiled grimly, remembering the brevity of Gload's summons, arriving six days into the old man's permanent and uninterruptible slumber: "Val, I'm ready for you now. In the tool shed in the Bag Balm can is everything you will need." It had come addressed simply to Deputy Valentine Millimaki, ATF, Cheyenne, Wyoming, and contained a check drawn on the Deer Lodge State Bank for $420.14. Note and check went into the hole. He had set the map aside in the long grass and now he took it up and threw it in. He stood for a long time with the wind cooling him and in the end he took the tiny silver charm on its silver chain from his pocket, weighed it in his palm and dropped it in.

Last he read the letter that had been written on yellow legal paper and folded and refolded until the page was small enough to fit through the hole in the top of the can:

Thanks for coming, Valentine. If you didn't come whoevers reading this can go ahead and burn the whole deal cause it won't make no sense but I figure you would. I told you Wexler was ambitious he could of turned these in to the Bull and that would of been that but he wanted the glory if thats what youd call it. Like I said About him. But now there yours and you can find some bones and everybodys happy. None of these is Wexler

just so you know. I knew you were tired of finding bones and
such so you can let the pogues at the Sheriffs take care of that
part Just a little payback for putting up with an old man You
were good to me Valentine. I hope you have a good life from
here on in.

Your FRIEND John X Gload

PS I was yours even if you wasnt mine.

He put the letter in his breast pocket along with the topographical maps similarly folded, on them five clear Xs noting the
location of graves in the breaks country north of the Missouri
River and of the smelterworks and the city. Nameless bones—
skulls without teeth, arms without hands—he knew would be
dredged from their repose to occupy another hole under other
stones, the plastic flowers planted there pale replicas of the wild
blooms of prairie spring.

He began to throw dirt into the hole when he heard clearly
then the high thin cry. He saw them drifting up from the river.
At first they seemed mere wisps of smoke, like traces of fireworks in the flat white sky but they came on, riding thermals
with infinitesimal movements of their chevron wings and soon
enough they became clear, their breasts the color of dirty bandages. They came nearer and began to circle, two or three. A
dozen. He dropped the shovel and moved into a clearing, his
arms upheld and waving like the limbs of the orchard trees
themselves. "Git," he called. He made shooing motions in the
air and looked like a man trying to rid himself of something.
He cried up at the birds. "Sonsofbitches. Git."

ACKNOWLEDGMENTS

My deep and lasting thanks to Dan Conaway, agent and friend; to Aaron Schlechter, for his intestinal fortitude; to Sarah Bowlin and her fine and talented colleagues at Holt. My gratitude extends miles in all directions for support and encouragement in the face of logic to Neil McMahon, Bill Kittredge, and friends and family who never stopped asking. I am grateful to my children for their sacrifice over the many years of my work. Thanks to Chuck Schuyler for legal insight and Jolanta Benal for her keen eye.

Special thanks to Mike Jaraczeski, ATF senior special agent, retired, for the many late-night, gin-fueled conversations that planted the seed.

And of course this book would not have happened without the enduring support, sensitive editing and beautiful poetic squint of my wife, Janet. It just flat wouldn't have.

ABOUT THE AUTHOR

Kim Zupan, a native Montanan, grew up in and around Great Falls, where much of the novel is set. For twenty-five years Zupan made a living as a carpenter while pursuing his writing. He holds an MFA from the University of Montana and has also worked as a smelterman, pro rodeo bareback rider, ranch hand, and Alaska salmon fisherman. Presently he teaches carpentry at the University of Montana's Missoula College. He lives in Missoula.